SUB-ZERO

Submariner Sinclair Series
Book Five

John Wingate

SAPERE
BOOKS

SUB-ZERO

Published by Sapere Books.

20 Windermere Drive, Leeds, England, LS17 7UZ,
United Kingdom

saperebooks.com

ISBN: 978-1-80055-285-2

To
E. P. W.

Some incidents in this book are true. All characters are fictitious, but if anyone who took part in similar wartime operations should recognise himself, the fact is coincidental and I offer my apologies.

The Author

THE SHIP'S COMPANY OF HIS MAJESTY'S
SUBMARINE *RUGGED*

Lieutenant Peter Sinclair, D.S.C., R.N., Commanding Officer

Lieutenant Tom Benson, D.S.C., R.N.R., First Lieutenant and Second-in-Command

Sub-Lieutenant Ian Taggart, R.N.R., Navigating Officer

Sub-Lieutenant Harold Spink, R.N., Third Hand and Torpedo Officer

Midshipman Michael O'Donovan, R.N., Fourth Hand and Gunnery Officer

Lieutenant Ewan Craig, R.N., Engineer Officer

Lieutenant Geoffrey Brocklebank, R.N., Electrical Officer

Lieutenant George ('Hank') Jefferson, D.S.C., U.S.N., United States Liaison Officer

C.P.O. George Withers, D.S.M., Coxswain

C.E.R.A. Reginald Potts, D.S.M., Chief E.R.A.

P.O. Jack Weston, D.S.M., Second Coxswain

P.O. James Haig, D.S.M., P.O. Telegraphist

P.O. Rodney Slater, D.S.M., Torpedo Instructor

E.R.A. Joseph Saunders, D.S.M., Outside E.R.A.

Acting-P.O. David Elliott, D.S.M., Higher S/M Detector

Leading Seaman Michael Flint, Leading Torpedoman

Leading Signalman Alec Goddard, Signalman

Able Seaman George Stack, Ex-Gunlayer and 'chef'

Alfred Bloom, Leading Seaman

Able Seaman William Hawkins, Seaman

Able Seaman Henry Bowles, Seaman

Ordinary Seaman Tom O'Riley, Ward Room Flunkey

Ordinary Seaman John Smith, T.I.'s Mate

S.P.O. George Hicks, Stoker Petty Officer

Stoker Patrick O'Connor, Stoker

Ordinary Seaman Leslie Thatcher, Telegraphsman and Telephone Operator

AUTHOR'S NOTE

For obvious security reasons, the correct technical ranks and rates have not been given in the nominal list. The ship's company have retained instead the titles to which they have been accustomed for so many years whilst serving in conventional submarines.

If the reader has followed Sinclair in the earlier books of the 'Submariner Sinclair' series, they will no doubt make allowances for the ageless quality of those who take part in these stories. The spirit of adventure is timeless, however, and the youth of today takes over from those who were young but yesterday…

CHAPTER 1

The Ghost

"I thought Kramer was dead."

The statement echoed round the high-ceilinged room and then, for a moment, there was silence. Behind the Admiralty desk sat Captain J. Croxton, D.S.O., D.S.C. and Bar. He was twiddling an ebony ruler between his fingers while he watched the two young men in front of him.

The speaker was the Englishman, a young man in his early twenties. His grey eyes were fixed upon his companion lolling in the other chair; a lanky American with a gaunt face, lean and spare.

"So did I, Pete. Shucks! The files give him as executed on 12th July, 1947, shortly after Nuremberg."

Captain Croxton, but recently Flag Officer Submarines, was now Deputy Director of Naval Intelligence.

"There are many curious records in the files, you know," he said, "von Kramer wasn't the only Nazi who swapped identities after the war." He rose from his desk, stretched himself and strode to the window overlooking The Mall. He motioned Sinclair and Jefferson to join him.

"Looks peaceful, doesn't it?" he mused, nodding at the neat rows of plane trees. They stood sentinel, their trunks mottled by the peeling bark and the sunlight filtering through the leaves. "On this June morning, you couldn't realise we are standing on the edge of a cataclysm."

Peter Sinclair, Lieutenant, Royal Navy, looked askance at his one-time Commanding Officer. Surely Joe wasn't losing his sense of proportion now he'd joined the ranks of the illustrious? It was an eternity since Joe Croxton had returned from the prisoner-of-war camp in Italy, after he had been sunk in *Restless* off Tunis. Peter had watched Joe being destroyed by the Italian hunters; the memory still haunted.

"What d'you mean, sir?" Peter asked.

Croxton's face was set when he turned towards his ex-First Lieutenant.

"Nothing is too improbable, Sinclair," he said. "There is so much spying and counter-espionage going on that nothing surprises me any longer. But there's something big going on and neither M.I.5 nor Admiralty know much about it."

"So you don't disbelieve me, sir?" Lieutenant George Jefferson, U.S.N., blurted.

"Why the hell d'you think I've sent for you two?" the captain asked, jutting his chin outwards in that characteristic manner which Peter knew too well. "For a game of uckers?"

Peter Sinclair smothered his grin: Croxton was on form.

"You're the only two men alive who knew what von Kramer was really like," Croxton continued. "So when Jefferson turns up and states categorically that he recognised this Nazi in Hamburg, I naturally follow it up. Kramer is such a high-calibre agent, as you well know from past experiences, that he'll slip through any net we cast. That's why you're here."

Peter Sinclair's heart sank. So this was why he'd been flown back from Flensburg, two days before the NATO exercises were due to begin. He'd left *Rugged*, his nuclear command, safely with Benson, his experienced First Lieutenant. Even if Peter could fly back tonight, he'd only have a day to check everything before the exercise started. And now *this*: they might even take him out of his beloved submarine and be made to join some N.I.D. stunt. Blast Kramer, blast 'em all…

"Don't look so chokka, Sinclair," Croxton said, reading his thoughts. "I'm not relieving you of your command."

Peter sighed. He knew he wasn't doing too well compared to some of the younger C.O.s. It was time some luck came his way: submariners were judged by results.

"Thank heavens, sir. Thought for a moment you were going to send me on some skylark."

Croxton smiled. "Not yet, Peter. We don't know enough: there's something going on we don't understand."

"And where there's Kramer there's trouble, you mean, sir?" Hank Jefferson asked, his brown eyes twinkling as he turned towards Peter. "I saw him in the docks in Hamburg when I landed, Pete. Looked as if he were boarding some sort of big cargo ship — *San Marco* was her name. She was flying the Panamanian flag. He recognised me, so I beat it."

"But are you *sure*, Hank?" Peter insisted. "He's a difficult brute to identify."

"Sure, Pete. It was old Ulrich himself, that no good—" Hank checked himself in the presence of his senior officer. "Heck, man, I ought to know, after Dubrovnik and the Citadel."

The two men looked at each other. They grinned as they remembered the agonies they had endured.

"All right, Hank, you win. So it *was* Kramer. What now?"

Croxton walked briskly back to his desk and sat down. He pressed the bell for his secretary.

"Sinclair, I'm not going into details, as Jefferson's told me all there is to know. You are to return to your submarine in Flensburg for the NATO exercise. Jefferson, you will return to Berlin and Hamburg and see what more you can discover. Next Friday evening you are both to join forces in Hamburg and see what more you can find out. I want Kramer identified beyond reasonable doubt. I must know what he's up to."

Peter shrugged his shoulders. What a commission!

"Where'll we meet, Hank?" he asked, disinterested in the whole proceedings. He itched to rejoin *Rugged*.

"By the bandstand in the Planten un Blomen."

"Where?" asked Peter incredulously.

"At nine-thirty on Friday night, 4th June, in the park of the Planten un Blomen. I ought to be there by then." Hank was grinning at his English friend.

"If you two have quite finished," Captain Croxton interrupted. "I'd like to get on with some work." He showed them the door. "And don't fail me, or I'll have you both court-martialled."

His eyes were twinkling as he pushed them out of his office. It was obvious, Joe thought, that Sinclair resented any job other than *Rugged*. He knew her ship's company so well now that the unit was shaken-down and efficient. It was surprising therefore that Sinclair had not had more luck after that West Indies affair. Since that extraordinary business, Sinclair had not shone as a C.O.; some of his contemporaries were already ahead of him in the promotion stakes. Croxton felt a sadness as his eyes travelled across the cream-painted ceiling, along the cornice and down the curtains to the window.

It did not seem long ago since he'd been sunk in *Restless*. Sinclair had tried to take some of the 'heat' upon himself by offering up the first *Rugged* as a decoy; but he'd been too late. It was a miracle that he, Croxton, had been picked up at all. Sometimes he wished that he hadn't been saved. He could never forget those first months in the prisoner-of-war camp: he'd wake with those nightmares, those dreadful ordeals in the middle of the night, when once again he relived the last minutes of *Restless*'s life. Nineteen of his men had been trapped below, while he, their war-weary Captain had been blown miraculously to the surface. Even now it did not make sense...

He'd been Sinclair's C.O. in the first *Rugged*, and though they'd shared the agony of wartime patrols from Malta, they'd also forged their comradeship. Sinclair, Jefferson and Hawkins (Arkwright was dead now) were the only people on our side of the fence who could recognise again that incredible man, Kramer: a sinister and able opponent if ever there was one. If Hank Jefferson had identified him there could be little doubt. Kramer had been found guilty after Nuremberg, but with his cunning and skill at disguise, it was not beyond the bounds of possibility that he'd escaped the gallows and lain low for all these years.

Yet, and yet...

Our agents were bringing in disquieting scraps of information, all related somehow to a resurgence of Nazism. Could Kramer's reappearance be in any way connected with these rumours? Disturbing, if it were so.

Well, he'd given Sinclair his chance — if he wanted his promotion he'd better seize the opportunity. Joe Croxton sighed as he moved again to the window. How he longed to be captain of a boat again, instead of being mixed up in this dirty game of espionage. Suddenly he was seeing no longer the dappled sunlight along the sides of The Mall. Instead, his mind wrestled with the miasma of distrust and hatred that was being engendered across the Channel. He felt like a man with the fog closing down upon him, a spring tide under him and the rocks ahead. Mortal danger, invisible, inaudible yet terrifyingly real.

CHAPTER 2

On the Billet

"Fog's closing in fast, sir."

Benson, First Lieutenant of H.M. Nuclear Submarine *Rugged*, turned from the periscope to report to his Captain. He had been with Sinclair now for some time: they instinctively knew each other's reactions. And now, looking at the Captain, a fair-haired man, grey-eyed and wiry of frame, Benson felt a deep bond between them. He realised that Peter Sinclair was not doing so well in the promotion stakes. There had been that day when he'd mistaken the Admiral's wife for someone else's; amusing at the time but, in these days of cut-throat competition, an incident like that could be disastrous. *Rugged* was in the British Section of the United Nations Naval Security Force and nothing had happened for months. And now fog was closing down to spoil their chances, even in a NATO naval exercise. Benson smoothed his black hair. He felt sorry for the Old Man.

"Up periscope."

The steel tube slid upwards until the Captain flicked his thumb above the handle. Silently the periscope slid to a stop. Peter Sinclair screwed his eyes into the face-piece. A quick all-round look, then he slammed shut the handles.

"All-round H.E. sweep."

"All-round H.E. sweep, sir," repeated Elliott, the black-haired H.S.D. from his Asdic cabinet. He crouched low over his set, intent on picking up the smallest sound. The hands in the Control Room watched him idly. The only sounds were the whining of the electric motors and the occasional rustle from the helmsman as he spun his wheel.

Peter Sinclair waited impatiently. He was fed up with this exercise. He'd flown back from London, just managing to catch *Rugged* in time. *Rugged*'s role was to be the end link in an 'Iron Ring' of submarines blockading the Skagerrak. No ship was to be allowed out of the Baltic. The West German Navy was representing the Russians. It was to escort a convoy and break out from the Baltic. And, Peter guessed, *Rugged* would never sight anything from her position at this southern end of the Iron Ring. In this fog and in these shallows, she dare not remain dived for fear of collision. What rotten luck…

"All-round H.E. sweep completed, sir. Nothing to report."

"Surface."

The Cox'n and Second Cox'n peered at their depth gauges, grasped their hydroplane handles more firmly. The outside E.R.A. checked all main vents shut.

"Blow one, blow six," snapped the First Lieutenant.

The high-pressure air screamed along the line, the Captain snapped his fingers and watched the periscope sliding from its well; there was a lifting beneath their feet as the bows came up and then she was sliding bodily upwards.

Peter stood by the periscope, right hand on the handle as he watched the pointers sliding round the dials. At forty-five feet he clamped his forehead against the rubber face-piece. Nothing, nothing but a dull greyness percolating down from the surface.

"Thirty-eight feet, sir," Benson reported from between the gauges.

Peter watched the upper lens breaking surface. The light streamed into his eyes as the water cleared from the glass; a moment while the wetness evaporated and then he could see.

He spun round the periscope, but only a few yards of grey sea undulated ahead of him. There was no horizon, only his restricted circle of vision merging into the fog. This was dangerous: better to be up top and able to use his surface radar to avoid collision. At full buoyancy *Rugged* would present a better target for any surface ship's radar. They would keep out of her way in this low visibility: it wasn't as if there were a war on — this was only an exercise.

He slammed shut the periscope handles and nodded at Number One. He started clambering up the conning tower, the brass rungs of the long ladder clammy cold beneath his grasp. Halfway up he could see Goddard's feet above him, the trusted signalman who always preceded him up the tower. Already he would be gripping the upper lid's clips, waiting for the order.

"Twenty-eight feet, sir."

Peter could hear Number One's report echoing from down below in the Control Room.

"Off one clip," Peter shouted upwards.

He heard the clatter of the long-handled clip as Goddard released it.

"Twenty feet, sir," from below.

"Open up!" Peter yelled.

The hatch flew open and suddenly there was a circle of daylight above his head. He clambered quickly up the last rungs of the ladder as Goddard scrambled through the upper lid.

Once on the dripping bridge, Peter moved quickly to the voicepipe. He yanked open the valve: he was now in communication with the Control Room. He heard Spink, the Officer of the Watch, puffing behind him.

"Keep your eyes skinned," Peter said. "We shan't get much warning if there's anything around." He turned to the voicepipe.

"Group up, slow ahead. Steer three-six-zero. Start all-round radar search on the surface scanner. Come to full buoyancy and flood 'Q'."

As the lookouts came up on the bridge to take up their positions, Peter smiled to himself. Lucky this wasn't the war. To be able to surface in daylight, use the radar scan in this area — what luxury! No exercise could reproduce the real thing.

But he was sure he was right in not risking his ship under these conditions. He must stay in the area and give warning of his position if any ship approached. With these tides and within seven miles of the Skagens, this was no place to be uncertain of one's position. Peter was idly peering through his glasses when he saw Spink's tall figure crouch over the voicepipe. He came over to the back of the bridge where Peter was standing.

"The Electrical Officer reports a fault on the surface scanner, sir. He thinks it's in the generator."

Peter swore softly. Why did these gadgets let you down when you needed them most? He moved to the voicepipe.

"Electrical Officer?"

"Yes, sir. Brocklebank speaking."

"How long will you be?"

"Can't say, sir, I'm afraid. It's a tricky one."

"Can I have the 247?" asked Peter. At least the attack radar would give him close-range warning.

"I'm afraid the fault is common to both, sir. The generator has reversed its polarity."

For a moment Peter said nothing. What was the point of an Electrical Officer if this sort of thing happened?

"All right, but hurry up. This is no place to be sitting starko on the surface."

"Sorry, sir. We'll do our damnedest."

Peter knew that Brocklebank was a tryer. These things happened to the best of submariners, but it was tricky just here, in these notorious waters. He remained at the fore-end of the bridge and spoke to the Officer of the Watch and the lookouts.

"Keep your eyes skinned: the radar's packed up. I don't want to be run down in this fog. Start the hooter, Officer of the Watch."

"Aye, aye, sir."

Spink leant over the voicepipe. "Air on the hooter. One long blast every minute."

Then there started the irritating wail of the air siren. The beast moaned through the fog and deafened everyone on the bridge. After an hour the noise was getting on their nerves.

The fog was thickening. Wads of it curled round the conning tower and blotted out the bows. The stuff clung to them and lay writhing upon the long, low swell.

Peter felt their own wind ruffling his hair but, except for the whisper of the sea curling along their pressure hull, there was a weird silence between the blasts of the hooter.

This had been an abortive week. The ridiculous visit to Admiralty, the rush back to *Rugged*, so that he'd been unable to prepare adequately for this exercise. If *Rugged* had not been such a compact and small submarine, she would have been useless on this billet. But these Mark IIs were fine boats: the direct conversion gear from nuclear to electrical energy had revolutionised the nuclear submarine. Without *Dreadnought*'s bulk, she still retained her predecessor's power and endurance. *Rugged* was small enough to operate in coastal waters, as her previous namesake had been. The only difference was her diving time. The *Rugged* that had worked out of Malta during the war could dive in eighteen seconds. It took the present forty-two seconds, but even this was a tremendous improvement on the first *Dreadnought*. However, as a nuclear normally never surfaced, there was no requirement for quick diving.

The lookout 'tricks' changed. Goddard went below for his dinner and Taggart, the Navigating Officer, relieved Spink. A hot mug of soup was handed through the upper lid and Peter was glad of its comfort. The fog was getting on his nerves now: he was hearing imaginary sirens in the lulls between his own hooter. He was glad to see Taggart.

"Got a good Decca fix, Pilot?"

The sandy-haired Scot from Montrose grinned at his Captain.

"Wouldn't like to bet on it, sir, but I think we're inside our billet. The last fix put us a mile and a half from our D.R."

"Good." Peter cocked his head suddenly. "D'you hear anything?"

Taggart turned his head towards the bows. "A ship — sounds close, sir."

Peter was tense. Was that the surge of a bow wave from somewhere right ahead? Must be very close — but why the devil wasn't she making fog signals?

"Sound the hooter!" Peter yelled down the voicepipe. "Collision stations!"

He pressed the collision alarm, and then, an instant later, he heard the doors slamming shut down below. He felt his heart hammering in his ears. This idiot was charging through the fog, without any sound signals. She must be a suicidal maniac…

Peter's immediate reaction was to dive.

"How much water under us, Pilot?" he snapped.

"About sixty feet, sir. I've just taken a sounding."

Peter leapt to the for'd end of the bridge. Was that a shape looming right ahead? It seemed to move down the port side, so close he could hear her fans running — like those of a destroyer. He heard voices in the fog, and then he saw a blurred outline leaning outwards as she turned. Only her stern was visible as she heeled over, half blanketed by the swirling fog.

"She's altering towards," Peter whispered. "She's deliberately trying to ram us, Pilot."

He lunged for the diving 'push'.

"Dive, dive, dive!" he yelled. "Clear the bridge."

He heard the main vents thunking open, saw the gouts of water spurting upwards through the vents; he leapt for the upper lid as Taggart's head disappeared. And then he saw a sight he would remember for the rest of his life.

Through the yellow-green of the fog swirling across the swell, a ghostly shape suddenly bore down upon them. At first a blur, then, as her bows scythed through the mist, the unmistakable outline of a destroyer's fo'c'sle. He could see her bridge now, compact, streamlined, two officers straining through binoculars, while another pointed towards the submarine. Suddenly the largest leant over. He bellowed downwards, his words floating across the gap of water. Even above the surge of her bow wave, Peter heard the German. He was paralysed by the sight of this destroyer, mesmerised by her stern cutting through the water. Her upperworks hung outwards over the water as she swung in a tight turn; but he could see no ensign, sight no pendant numbers. She was a modern destroyer, swift and powerful. And she was bent on destroying *Rugged*.

Peter heard the water gurgling through the free-flood holes, felt it splashing about his ears. With a sinking heart he grabbed the long-handled clip of the hatch. Even as he swung off into the gloom of the conning tower, his feet clambering for the rungs of the ladder, he knew that here he would be caught; here, in this iron coffin, the water cascading in upon him as the destroyer ripped her open. He felt his fingers tearing for the clip...

"First clip on!" he yelled breathlessly. "Sixty feet, but keep her tail down, for God's sake!"

He snapped home the second clip. He started slipping down the ladder, already a difficult feat with this steep bow-down angle. How the devil *could* Number One take her down fast, without this steep angle? He slithered down the last ten feet and sprawled into the Control Room.

Controlled pandemonium was reigning. To make themselves heard above the rumble of the attacking destroyer, the orders were being shouted. Number One stood feet astride between the planesmen, one hand flicking the pump-order instrument, the other holding on to the ladder for support. He snapped at the planesmen, trying to take the angle off her. At the after-planes sat the Cox'n, calm and grim as he wrestled with the 'bubble'. On the panel was the Outside E.R.A., Saunders, pale and wide-eyed as his hands snaked over the valves.

The compartment was sealed off now from its neighbour by the watertight doors. And all round them this holocaust, growing harsher at every second.

Peter daren't look at the depth gauges. There was thirty-three feet on the gauge as he fell into the Control Room. She must be ripped open at any second now. Forty-two, forty-three, forty —

Then she was struck.

It seemed to him at first that the curved frames were buckling inwards. Her whole side sprang towards him. He heard men gasping behind him, saw Benson turning hopelessly towards him. He watched the pointers jump on the gauges and then, as he grabbed the ladder for support, the main lighting dimmed, flickered for a second, went out.

She started rolling then, to starboard, then back to port, so fiercely that in the blackness it seemed she must be on her beam ends. But pervading the clatter and crashing of loose gear was the swish-swish of the propellers scything above them, the cacophony of her water noises and the pounding of her engines.

As she thundered overhead, *Rugged*'s bows struck bottom. At the same instant she broke free from her adversary; they were catapulted upright so that men were flung back to the starboard side.

Peter shut his eyes. The deluge of cascading seawater must overwhelm them now, mercifully ending their ordeal by drowning rather than by gassing from the chlorine that must soon envelop them. The battery cells must be cracked, and the seawater would do the rest; an oily green wisp of gas curling upwards from the boards and that would be all... Then the emergency lights snapped on.

Men with terror in their eyes gazed upwards towards the deckhead. But still no deluge... She must have struck another compartment ... it was too much to expect that she could have escaped damage to the pressure hull. How could they get out?

Each compartment had an escape hatch, it was true, but there was little future if drowning in the swirling tide was the alternative. And how long to hold on? How long would the air last?

The destroyer's H.E. disappeared on the port quarter while Peter waited for the boat to settle on the bottom. Still no water in the Control Room. He thrust his hands behind his back to control the trembling.

He nodded at the telegraphsmen. "All compartments make your reports," he ordered.

CHAPTER 3

Planten un Blomen

From the collision position to Kiel dockyard was two hundred and fifty-three miles. H.M. Nuclear Submarine *Rugged* entered the Kieler Bucht at twenty minutes past three during the afternoon of Thursday, June 3rd. It was a miracle that the pressure hull had remained intact; she had surfaced without incident an hour after the underwater collision.

Peter had been relieved to find the fog dispersing when he surfaced. Visibility had increased to a mile, and, as he clambered through the upper lid, he was astonished by the small amount of damage. Evidently the after jumping-wire had fouled their attacker (probably snarled around his A-bracket) and this had caused the terrifying list. A corner had been torn off the port fin but, apart from the length of jumping-wire trailing over the hull, there was no further damage. It had been fortunate that Peter had surfaced stern first or he might have fouled his own propeller.

He smiled to himself while he waited for a pilot at the entrance to the Kiel estuary. Joe Croxton would be the only senior officer in Admiralty who would credit the signal he had dispatched immediately after surfacing.

IMMEDIATE. TOP SECRET. To Flag Officer Submarines
Repeated Director of Naval Intelligence from Nuclear Submarine
Rugged.

Deliberately repeat deliberately savaged in low visibility 360 Skagens Light 7 miles by unidentified frigate, believed German. Request immediate investigation.

Am returning forthwith Kiel to effect superficial repairs to jumping wire and port fin. 220623.

As the pilot drew alongside beneath *Rugged*'s towering fin, Peter looked down sardonically. His signal would stir up a hornets' nest on the diplomatic front. Though Joe Croxton would support him, he doubted whether anything would come of the enquiry. No one must hurt the Germans' feelings these days. Yet a niggling idea had started to gnaw at the back of his mind. He dare not share his doubts with anyone other than Joe Croxton, and it would be some time before he could get him on a 'scrambler' line.

Could Kramer somehow have been behind the ramming incident? Supposing that Kramer had a network of agents infiltrated into the U.N.O. and NATO machines? A system that permeated even the communications and intelligence branches? It would then have been a routine matter for them to pick up Hank Jefferson's original signal to D.N.I., identifying von Kramer and requesting a meeting with Lieutenant Sinclair.

If they had in fact achieved this, then, for a man like Kramer, with his powerful network, it was not difficult to discover that Sinclair could now know of his existence. If therefore Kramer could eliminate Sinclair, the one man alive who could identify him beyond doubt, and who understood instinctively the intricate workings of his mind, then the danger of exposure would be removed. And if Kramer's influence extended amongst the officers in the West German forces, some of whom could have been undercover, unrepentant Nazis, then it would have been easy to detail a frigate to shadow *Rugged* on her billet. And, with a sympathetic C.O. aboard this frigate, what could have been simpler than to attempt a ramming, particularly in fog?

As the pilot shepherded *Rugged* slowly into the gigantic dockyard, this idea took root in Peter's mind. He'd try to get Joe Croxton on the 'scrambler' tomorrow night, after the rendezvous with Hank Jefferson in the park at Hamburg.

Rugged came gently alongside the brick wall where the U-boats had been built during the war. The rows of crane gantries stretched in martial efficiency into the distance. Already a brow was being swung out by a crane. Peter shook hands with the pilot, gave Benson his orders and made sure an armed sentry was being placed at the gangway. He changed into plain clothes, then went ashore.

After calling at the Naval Office to set in motion the arrangements for the repairs to *Rugged*, he walked to the dockyard gate where he asked the police the way to the railway station. He wanted the times of the trains for Hamburg. Tomorrow he would be meeting Hank, and he smiled at the thought. He was looking forward to propounding his suspicions, though he would have liked to have shared his secret with Benson. It was going to be difficult tomorrow, explaining his visit in plain clothes to Hamburg. He'd leave *Rugged* in Benson's capable hands: Number One could chase the dockyard as ably as he could. At the outside, the job should not take more than forty-eight hours.

On the diesel express to Hamburg, Peter woke only when it jolted to a halt in Neumunster. (He had spent forty-six hours on the bridge on passage from the Skagens.) He woke again as the train clattered over the points outside Hamburg station. He collected his grip and squared himself off in the mirror above the seat. He had tried to look as unlike an Englishman as possible: he wore his sports coat and grey flannels, but carried no hat. He smiled as he looked at the scruffy image: his face needed a shave, and he detested the German tie he sported. The grey plastic mac he had bought for a song gave him the colourless air of the Northern German. There were lines between his eyebrows, he noticed, and his grey eyes looked tired. The lean look on his face was accentuated by his pallor. He sighed. He could do with a rest, he thought, as he tried to persuade a parting in his tousled brown hair.

As he raised his arm he noticed a pair of blue eyes watching him from behind an opened *Frankfurter Allgemeine*. The man had sat in the opposite corner since Kiel, and had even offered Peter a cigar. Now their eyes met, and for an instant Peter caught the spark of hostility: a gaze that seemed to be memorising every facet of Peter's appearance.

Peter swung about. The paper rustled, and the man in the corner folded over the pages deliberately, without haste. Peter felt ridiculous as he reached for his grip.

"*Auf wiedersehen,*" the fair-haired man said.

His gold teeth flashed. Peter nodded and followed the other passengers from the compartment. He swung down on to the spotless platform of Hamburg station.

He looked over his shoulder. There was no sign of the man in his compartment. Peter shrugged his shoulders and swore at himself. He joined the orderly queue through the ticket barrier and enquired of the man behind him the way to the Planten un Blomen Park. His gaze idly travelled towards the carriage he had just quit. The fellow traveller was half-turned towards Peter and was standing by a pillar; his hands were cupped as he was lighting another cigar.

Peter hurried from the station. He jumped into a shiny red taxi. "Hotel-Pensionen Günther Hof, Reinfeldstrasse," he said.

The driver nodded and let in the clutch. The taxi slid from the kerb and accelerated smoothly. Peter glanced through the car window. The fair-haired man was walking towards the next taxi in the rank.

Peter felt his heart sink. Was he being followed? If so, he must have been tailed since setting foot ashore yesterday. Kramer's network must percolate through the whole German machine, in that case, and if Peter was to meet Hank in less than two hours' time, the rendezvous must be effected secretly.

He snatched at his wallet and delved for the small map of Hamburg. The pension was in Reinfeldstrasse, near the Planten un Blomen. The other taxi had not overhauled them yet. There was just time to throw off his shadower.

He leant forward and tapped on the window when the taxi slowed to enter Monckebergstrasse. He pointed to the left.

"Schwanenwik," he shouted.

The driver smiled, turned left and accelerated. As the cab cut back behind the mainline station, Peter glimpsed through his side window the shadowing taxi. It was swaying outwards as it turned right with the traffic streaming into the centre of the city.

Peter leaned back and sighed. He hated this game of cat and mouse: he could never have made a secret agent. He liked things in the open. A straightforward torpedo attack was more in his line.

He knew he had been followed. He couldn't explain the feeling, but he was certain this grinning German was a hired agent, paid to trail him. But at least Peter had thrown him off. He'd take a look at the lake of the Aussen Alster, then drive back to the pension, where Hank might have arrived already. If

Hank wasn't there, there'd be time for Peter to find his room, clean up and have a bite before meeting him at 9.30 in the park. He'd try to get there early, because Hank's timing could be erratic. The trip from Berlin could be anything but punctual with the red tape at the checkpoints.

Twilight was fading when Peter jumped from the bus that put him down outside the north-western entrance to the Planten un Blomen, Hamburg's famous exhibition park. His spirits were high. He'd be meeting Hank soon, that irrepressible Yank who'd shared so much with him in the past. Peter had jettisoned that ridiculous depression and fear he'd experienced during the train journey: he was jumpy from fatigue and Joe Croxton's fears, that was all. The incident of the fair-haired Hun was imagination, and he chuckled as he clicked his way through the turnstile underneath the sodium lights.

He stood in an open space from which the avenues diverged through the magnificent park. Paths curled through clouds of brilliant tulips, then were lost in the banks of vivid azaleas, dark clusters of shrubs and clumps of trees. All was bathed in a warm orange light, while the paths which disappeared through the shrubs and trees were illuminated by strings of fairy lanterns. He hesitated and looked about him. Where was the bandstand? From the map by the turnstile there was one by this north-western entrance and one by the south-eastern gate. Hank had not specified which.

Peter joined the trickle of humanity converging towards the music which thumped from behind a clump of trees ahead of him. He found himself in a clearing, in the centre of which was the circular bandstand. Rows of tiered benches surrounded the bandsmen who were dressed in dark green, with yellow trimmings. Peter smiled. The Germans loved uniforms, but at least they looked less hot than some of the perspiring municipal musicians.

A large crowd jostled around the space between the benches and the foot of the bandstand. Families had brought their evening meal and there they sat in the cool, munching their sausage and downing their beer.

Peter worked his way to the edge of the circle, by the exit that led to the other side of the park. From here he could watch both approaches. If Hank intended this bandstand, Peter would see his arrival. He'd wait here until a quarter to ten before trying the other bandstand. He settled his back against a tree trunk and crossed his legs.

At first he didn't notice them. The resumption of the music, the happiness of the multitude around him had made him drowsy. But then he became aware of a group of louts on the far side of the bandstand. They looked an unpleasant lot, tough and ruthless — hardly a group likely to enjoy Tchaikovsky. They were probably here to chase the girls, he thought. A bunch of 'Teds', out for trouble. Every nation seemed cursed by this pathetic flotsam.

Yet this group seemed different. The leader was much older: about thirty, Peter thought, as he glanced at the rowdy bunch. More a Pole than a German. With his wide eyes, fair hair, high cheekbones and wide, Slavonic mouth he was a tough-looking brute. The man seemed to be briefing the thugs grouped silently around him. For an instant Peter caught the leader glancing across at him ... and then, one by one, each of the gang (about nine or ten of them, Peter thought), casually turned towards him.

Peter looked quickly about him. There was no one behind his tree. If these thugs were out to beat him up, he could bolt down this path leading through the shrubbery. It was dark in there. He felt his heart thumping against his ribs as the band stopped suddenly.

The loudspeakers in the trees crackled: "*Achtung, achtung!*" an announcer interrupted in a metallic voice. "Here is a message for Herr Sinclair. Herr Sinclair from Herr Jefferson. Please meet him at the south-east gate, at the south-east gate. "*Danke schön.*"

The band struck up once more. The lights dimmed. A blue light shone upon the faceless audience. Yet, concealed in this crowd, there could be ten vicious hoodlums, bent perhaps, on doing him no good. Why so many — and apparently ready for him?

Without waiting to find out, Peter slipped from the tree trunk. He darted down the pathway, disappearing into the tunnel of rhododendrons and shrubs.

It was dark in here, pitch black after the arena around the bandstand. This tunnel seemed to be bored out of a solid mass of shrubs. He moved quickly, feeling his way through the blackness. His heart was hammering, and he knew he was scared. A path crossed from right to left and he darted swiftly across. He stopped then, listening…

Was that a pattering, a rustle from the path to his right? Above the bumping of his heart he could hear nothing … but suddenly he heard guttural German, low and urgent, from the darkness on the right.

He broke into a run, then, for the first time, he glanced over his shoulder as the leaves brushed his face. He turned and ran, and then a faint blue light flickered ahead. Ah! He'd be through in a moment, saved by the lights. Then suddenly it was brighter. Only one corner to round. He dashed into the light. There was the damnable bandstand he'd left a few minutes earlier. And on the far side, covering the exit he had left, a gigantic man … waiting…

Peter was too slow. The commotion he made caught the attentions of the tough who was now shambling towards him. Peter doubled back into the tunnel.

He began running and, when he looked back, he saw a torch beam behind him. Then somewhere ahead of him he heard subdued voices and the sound of padding feet. He gained the first crossing, then heard a shout behind him. A call answered from right ahead. His skin began prickling at the back of his neck; already he could feel the steel sliding between his shoulder blades…

Then he saw red. Who the devil were these people anyway? And what were they playing at? Was he, P. Sinclair, to be bullied and chivvied by a bunch of hoodlums? Though he was not even armed he became suddenly very angry. He turned left and threw himself into the left-hand wall of the shrubbery tunnel. He pulled the foliage across him.

He remained motionless, as still as his breathing would allow. Then, as a torch beam came abreast of him, he held his breath. One snap of a twig and —

His pursuer had paused at the junction of the paths. In the beam of the light Peter could distinguish his features: a huge man, hunched and crouching to spring, with arms hanging like a gigantic ape. In his right hand the blade of a knife flashed. The lout looked down the main route, paused, swung the torch beam down the tunnel. Peter saw the beam shining upon the leaves opposite. *Dear God, make him take the other path…*

The beam flickered, went out. The man loped down Peter's track, then paused two yards away. Peter, his nerves taut, flexed his knees to spring, slowly raised his arms to parry that terrible knife. He held his breath. The man was looming towards him…

The thug peered back over his shoulder as he passed; he was looking to his right, searching the junction of the paths with his torch beam, his back towards Peter. His teeth were bared, the lips drawn back tightly; a savage beast with murder in his heart. Peter sprang with all his strength.

The man jerked towards the rustle, presenting a full target as he raised his striking arm. Peter, with the weight of his body behind him, smashed his left fist squarely into the devil's face. At the same instant, he grabbed at the man's right wrist.

There was a grunt. The torch jerked into the foliage, went out. Peter's knee came up hard into the brute's stomach. His assailant gasped, there was a choking sob and the human mass crumpled to the ground.

The blood felt wet on Peter's wrist. His mind racing, he knew now his life was at stake. Lights were flickering on the far side of the junction and there was a hubbub of subdued Teutonic commands. He was trapped. There was only one way out.

He rolled the senseless man into the undergrowth. He doubled back on his tracks. He reached the junction and, sobbing from fear and exhaustion, he raced through the darkness, back towards the bandstand from which he had started.

He glanced back over his shoulder when he reached the last curve, where the lights were infiltrating through the leaves. He gasped in relief — there was no sign of his pursuers — and when he collected himself at the last bend, he could see no one watching the exits now.

He mingled with the crowd listening to the band. He edged round to the main exit, and was once more under the glare of the arc lights. He glanced down at his clothes, brushed off the dirt and strode to the exit. The attendant looked curiously at him, the stile clicked and Peter was again in the Rentzelstrasse. No shadowy figures here. He stretched his shoulders, took his bleeding left hand from his pocket, sucked the raw knuckles and turned right, down the Tiergartenstrasse.

It was safer here, in this wide street running along the railway line. If he kept to his right, he could enter the Planten un Blomen by the south-eastern gate, while the hoodlums were still searching the maze in the shrubbery.

Hank should be waiting here. With his six-feet four, he would be a comfort to have around. It could be no more than fifteen minutes since the announcement. Hank would wait some time before returning to the pension. Then a suspicion flickered through Peter's mind: an extraordinary coincidence, the loudspeaker announcement and the killer mob.

He kept close to the wall as he entered the Bei den Kirchhöfen. There was the entrance a few hundred yards ahead. He'd have to pay his entrance again, damn it — perhaps the Navy would reimburse him. He could nip inside and take a quick look at the other bandstand. His enemy wouldn't be expecting him at this entrance.

The bleeding of his knuckles had ceased now that he had bound them with his handkerchief, but he kept his left hand in his pocket as he clicked through the turnstile. Ah! There was the bandstand, right ahead of him, the band thumping away briskly. From the shadow beneath this kiosk he could watch unobserved.

No sign of Hank. But he'd feared this development since he escaped from the other end of the park. The announcement on the loudspeaker had either been a hoax, or Hank had tired of waiting and had returned to the Günther Hof Pension.

Peter walked through the exit turnstile. The officials were scratching their heads. Crazy, some people, they were obviously thinking…

Peter quickened his step. He'd find Hank waiting at the pub. He was sure of that; quite certain…

CHAPTER 4

Pursuit

Peter was halfway up the first flight of stairs in the hotel when the proprietor hailed him from the hall. With an ingratiating manner, he was rotund, with piggy eyes and rimless spectacles.

"Herr Sinclair?"

"Yes."

"Herr Jefferson not back with you?"

"No."

Peter watched the man carefully. He mistrusted every strange face now, but there'd been no one shadowing the hotel.

"You will excuse me, *mein Herr*." The round face was expressionless as he spoke in the North German dialect, "but Herr Jefferson left with two other friends who called for him. He did not say where he was going. He seemed very silent." The man's stubby fingers scratched his bald cranium.

"Go on, please," Peter said quietly, in German.

"Though he said nothing, *mein Herr*, I had the feeling he wanted to speak. It seemed he was…" the German faltered and averted his eyes.

"Frightened?"

"Terrified, *mein Herr*. He's a big man to be frightened."

Peter was silent. He'd never seen Hank scared in all the years he'd known him.

"What were his friends like?"

"They seemed quiet enough. They asked for yours and Herr Jefferson's room. They went straight upstairs. They did not even take off their coats."

"Did they say where they were going? Leave any message?"

"Nothing, *mein Herr.*"

"If there's a phone call for me, *mein Herr*, please don't accept it. Make any excuse."

"You are out?"

Peter smiled. "No, *mein Herr*. Please say that I do not wish to be disturbed until the morning. Now, if you'll excuse me…"

The German hotelier smirked. The lenses in his spectacles were glinting under the light.

"Good night, *mein Herr*. I hope you sleep well."

Peter nodded and smiled. It had been a long day; he was tired.

"Goodnight."

He climbed slowly up the stairs to his room on the second floor. Who could these men have been? It was unlikely that Hank would bring friends on this jaunt. He flung open the door of his room.

He glanced round the tiny apartment. Spotlessly clean, nothing out of place, nothing ransacked, though the curtains were drawn. Hank would have left some clue if he'd been kidnapped. He would have fought for it if he'd had half a chance.

Peter threw himself on his bed. They'd booked this room for secrecy. And now Hank had been hijacked — Hank of all people… He couldn't believe it.

Pull yourself together. No ruddy panic. Whoever are the enemy, work fast. They've tried to murder me. Maybe they've kidnapped Hank from this very room. There must *be a reason for all this…*

He lay on the bed, his hands behind his head. *Think, man, think. What was the cause of all this? Must be a case of mistaken identity. Why, for goodness sake?* And then he wrenched his mind back to their meeting in Joe Croxton's Admiralty office.

Kramer had been recognised by Hank. No doubt about it. Hank could have been recognised by Kramer. So far so good. If Kramer was reacting as violently as this, something of extreme importance must be in the wind, the secrecy of which was vital to Kramer.

Fine. That made sense. But where was Kramer? It wasn't too circumstantial to assume that the two thugs who had abducted Hank had taken him to Kramer who must therefore be somewhere in Hamburg.

His heart was racing. He'd better quit this place before *they* called for him also. He swung off the bed and went to collect his shaving things from the wash basin in the corner. He stopped in his tracks as he read the soap message smeared across the mirror:

GET OUT OF HAMBURG OR AMERICAN KAPUT

Underneath, a swastika surrounded by a circle; that evil, crooked cross…

Damn them. Blast their brazen effrontery. They must be pretty powerful if they could throw their weight about like this, in the middle of Hamburg. They'd kill Hank anyway, just as they tried to fix him. Kramer's word was valueless, let alone his henchmen's.

He grabbed his things and tossed them into his grip. Evidently they'd allowed Hank to take his gear with him. But how was he to get out of the pub? They must be watching it.

He slowly opened the door. He peeped across the landing. No one about. He slipped to the landing below. As he expected, its window overlooked the frontage of the hotel. The landing light was controlled from below, and this had not been switched on. He slipped quietly to the side of the window and, flattening himself against the wall, peered out.

It took several minutes for his eyes to adjust themselves to the darkness. And then he saw them — two men at either end of the block, both in the shadows.

He felt the fear seeping through him again. These thugs were ruthless, of the flick knife variety. A cold, murderous game this: no quarter could be expected from them … and Peter had nothing with which to defend himself.

It would be suicide to walk out of the front door. He slipped across the landing to the rear face of the building. There must be a fire escape somewhere; the Germans were an efficient people. Ah! There it was. He could see it through this back window, but how to reach it? His eyes followed the steel steps upwards, until they curled out of sight above his head: must start somewhere on the roof. All right, nothing else for it.

He nipped upstairs and slipped back into his room. No one had seen him so far. He slumped on the bed for a moment to recover himself. He was frightened, he had to admit it. Though he didn't know where they'd taken Hank, the first priority was to elude this trap — he could always go to the British Consulate or the police.

Or could he? Joe Croxton insisted that this business was top secret. If he threw himself on the mercy of the authorities, the lid would be blown off … it would end his career anyway. What a mess… To get out of here quickly, that was all that mattered.

He left enough money on the bedside table to pay for his room. He'd take a last look round before locking the door behind him. (He could send the key back through the post if he was alive to do so.)

He opened the drawers in the wardrobe from habit. For once, he'd forgotten nothing. He glanced between the beds. *Hullo, what was this?*

On the floor was a Bible, obviously dropped by mistake. It was lying open, and Peter picked it up carefully. It was one of those given to hotels by the missionary societies and it was open at the first page of the Gospel of Saint Mark. And there, as if a thumbnail or some sharp instrument had gouged into it, was a ragged indentation beneath the capitals, SAINT MARK.

A message from Hank? Peter unzipped his grip and pushed the Bible inside. He opened the door a crack. The landing was deserted. He slipped out of his room.

He locked the door, dropped the key into his pocket and slipped silently up to the darkness of the floor above. Another four bedrooms, but leading up from this floor was an uncarpeted staircase into what was probably the staff quarters in the attics. The fire escape must start from there. At this time of night the maids wouldn't yet be off duty. He nipped up the few remaining stairs. By the glow of the light from below he could see a trapdoor in the ceiling and a ladder on a pulley leading up to it. He gingerly lowered the wooden ladder; the squeak of the pulleys made his heart leap. Someone must be disturbed soon...

He clambered up through the trapdoor. He hauled the ladder after him and belayed the rope round its own part, making it up carefully so that no ends were dangling. He lowered the trapdoor gently back into position. He was now in the loft, and in the darkness he sighed with relief. Safe so far: now to reach the roof and find the fire escape.

A skylight was directly overhead: the glass allowed a square of pale light to filter through from the city outside. Peter grasped the skylight and lifted its lower edge. He felt the night air on his face and saw the stars above him. He looped one handle of his grip over his shoulder and scrambled upwards until he could squat up on the lower ledge of the skylight. He was breathing deeply from the exertion, yet had made little noise. He folded back the skylight and took his bearings.

Above him the ridge of the roof ran horizontally across the night sky, the glow from the city looming up from below. A yard below him stretched the guttering of the roof; wooden laddering led over the tiles down to the fire escape which began here. Peter had only to nip on to the steel fire escape and he was away. Yet some instinctive caution that comes to those who have lived long with physical danger, some intangible sixth-sense, held him back.

Until now the invisible enemy had been jumps ahead, had anticipated every movement of Hank's and his. Their adversaries seemed to have considerable resources. They would not be watching only the front of the hotel.

He peered over the edge, down to the darkness below: he must be a good eighty feet up, though in the darkness he could barely see the strip of darkness behind the hotel. Beyond the garden wall stretched an avenue of trees, the light from street lamps flickering through the leaves. Beyond that wooden fence, he must presume that more of the enemy lurked.

It started to rain as he stared along the roof. The hotel building seemed to be one in the middle of a crescent. He smiled as he remembered Southsea, that architectural haven of boarding houses. If this pub had an escape, presumably the others must also have one. He dared not take this obvious escape, down this hotel's ladder. There was nothing for it but to risk a sortie along the roof to the other end of the row. There *must* be another escape at the far end.

Peter did not like heights. As a midshipman, he had had to conquer the terror that swamped him if he looked downwards. And now in the darkness he was forced to crawl across these wet slates to the far end, a good forty yards. If only he could reach the ridge of the roof — but he'd be silhouetted against the night sky. He heard then a commotion and guttural shouting somewhere below him...

With his heart hammering in his ears, he lifted his legs over the ledge, lowered the skylight behind him and sat with his heels pushing against the guttering. Gingerly he started to edge himself along the tiles.

Slowly, gently, he levered himself away from the skylight. A foot at a time, with death yawning in the darkness below, he edged himself along, the tiles greasy and as slippery as ice; and at the back of his mind, the fear of the guttering being rotten and collapsing beneath his weight.

He had gained ten yards now, ten yards nearer safety, when suddenly his right heel slipped. He smothered the cry that escaped through his lips. He sat there a moment, to conquer the trembling that had gripped his limbs. Then he saw the torch beam flickering in the hotel garden he had just left so hurriedly.

He tore off his shoes, and with one hand slipped them into his grip which hung, a dead weight, from his right shoulder. He forced himself onwards, knowing that each yard was another farther from capture. Then at last he could see the endcoping of the final house at the end of the crescent, only twenty feet away. And to his joy there were the iron bars of another fire escape almost within reach. He increased the pace and suddenly, in his carelessness, dislodged a broken piece of tile. It slithered and clattered across the tiles. He held his breath as he waited for it to go hurtling over the edge to crash in the darkness below... He shut his eyes and waited, waited, blood pumping in his ears. *This was it then: the swine would be waiting for him at the bottom of the fire escape; they would mount the ladder to meet him and shoot him down in cold blood. The silencers would make little noise in the darkness...* He waited, tensed and nerves quivering up there in the terror of the night.

Then slowly into his numbed brain came the realisation that no sound had shattered this silence. Nothing yet but the distant roar of the traffic, the patter of the rain on the tiles. He opened his eyes and looked along the guttering. There was the fragment of broken tile, caught in the gutter and balanced precariously between earth and sky, the arbiter of fate for P. Sinclair.

Peter pulled himself together. These agonising minutes had tested him: he'd vanquished the fear now. If he'd reached as far as this, the good God must be on his side. He edged towards the broken tile until his left foot was within inches of it, leant over the darkness with his left hand and gently closed his fingers around it. His fingers trembled as he slipped the tile into a coat pocket. Then with two more heaves he was alongside another skylight and immediately above the other fire escape. He edged over the guttering and lowered his feet gingerly on to the steel plating of the ladder. He felt the rigidity taking his weight and for a moment he leant against the guard rail to recover his equilibrium. His arms ached and his legs were trembling. He'd never felt such an idiot.

He looked back whence he'd come. The torch beam had left the garden but suddenly a light glowed through the hotel skylight. He ducked beneath the guttering as he watched the light shining through the pane of glass. So they had guessed his moves, had they, followed him as far as the skylight? He'd left no clue behind him; his thoughts raced as he lay on the wet steel footplate in the darkness. He'd even secured the trapdoor ladder as he'd found it. They couldn't believe he'd climbed along this roof in the darkness. And yet...

He cautiously raised his head above the guttering. The skylight was open. He could see plainly the silhouette of a man etched against the beam of light in the sky. He was gazing downwards at the hotel ladder and held a torch in his hand. Suddenly the beam started to swing across the roof towards Peter. He saw the gleam of wet tiles and he dropped his head again into the shadows.

He held his breath. This was a moment of finality. Either the man would conclude that no fool would venture along the roof in these conditions or else he'd decide that it was a possible feat. In that case they'd come for him up the remaining fire escape. Peter crouched in the shadows, calming the terror in his heart. He forced himself to wait five minutes before looking again. Then he slowly raised his head.

There was no light from the hotel skylight. A sigh escaped him. He extracted his shoes and slipped them on. Then he pattered down the outside fire escape, a spiral affair made of latticed ironwork. He passed the dim light of curtained windows as he regained ground level. Then at last he was standing on a concrete back yard. Mercifully there was no dog. He slipped down the garden path that led to the back gate in the wooden fence running alongside the street.

He hesitated, his finger resting on the latch of the gate. Once through here, he would be in the glare of the street lighting: they might still be watching…

The latch was lifting slowly against the pressure of his own finger. His heart leapt into his mouth. He slid behind the door. He crouched in the shadows of the shrubs growing there. In the darkness the scent of rosemary was sweet in his nostrils. He lowered his grip gently to the ground and waited with clenched fists. The door was opening slowly, creaking on its hinges.

CHAPTER 5

The San Marco

Hank Jefferson, D.S.C., Lieutenant United States Navy, woke shortly before dawn on June 4th. Grey fingers were streaking the eastern sky. The pale light seemed colder through the tiny scuttle, his only contact with the outside world in this cramped cell.

He gingerly felt the lump on the side of his head. His head still ached from the blow they'd given him as soon as they'd got him out of sight below *San Marco*'s bulwarks. His mouth twisted with bitterness as he recalled the events of last night.

After the two thugs had surprised him in the Hotel Günther Hof, they had bustled him out at gunpoint into the waiting car. Ten minutes later they were passing through the dock gates, but though they had gagged him in the back of the car, he had recognised where they were absconding with him: down to number one-three-seven billet, the inshore berth of the Sandtorhafen.

He smiled ruefully in his cramped cell. He ought to know this berth, for Pete's sake: he'd been watching it for two days from a park bench amongst the flower beds of St. Annen Platz. It was here that he'd first bumped into von Kramer. The Nazi had dismissed his car in the Platz so that he could walk unobtrusively the remainder of the distance. If they had not recognised each other then, Hank would not be lying here with a blacksmith's anvil ringing between his temples.

The pain grew worse, the angrier he became. The memory of the swine who'd crept up and coshed him sent the anvils ringing overtime. Now he'd woken in this cell, with its tiny, barred scuttle.

He glanced at his watch: a quarter past five. The piles of the jetty were green with slime and oil-soaked. It must be shortly after low-water because the scuttle was rubbing against the barnacles at the bottom of the piles. The ship would be beginning to float upwards again. High-water about eleven thirty, then.

He began to pull himself together and to take stock of his surroundings. He slipped from the canvas cot-bunk and gingerly took his weight on his feet. He shook himself to clear his swimming senses, clutching the steel handle of the cell door for support. The rattle brought a muffled Teutonic oath from outside.

A German seaman opened the door. He covered Hank with a Tommy gun. His eyes were fixed on Hank. His fingers were on the trigger. "What d'you want?" he growled in German.

Hank rubbed his head where the blood had congealed. He slowly shook his head from side to side.

"Cigarette, *bitte*," Hank asked quietly. Anything to ease the pain.

The sailor looked a decent sort; straightforward, disciplined, no-nonsense type. For a moment he stood motionless. Then, decency overcoming his training, he slipped the gun to his right hand. Still covering Hank, he removed with his left hand his cap with its gold-lettered ribbon: *San Marco*. He tossed its contents into the cell and kicked the door. It swung shut.

"*Danke schön*," Hank yelled.

"*Danke bitte*," came the muffled reply from outside.

Sailors are the same the world over, Hank thought. *Soft hearts, some of 'em, beneath a rough surface.* He bent down to retrieve from the deck the half-used cigarette packet and a box of matches. He clambered back to his canvas bunk; lay back to ease the pain.

He lit a cigarette, felt the pleasure of the weed. He watched the smoke spiralling upwards towards the ventilator in the deckhead. At least he wasn't going to fumigate himself to death: this must be an old ship, with old-fashioned, mushroom-shaped vents. He pulled at the cigarette and felt his brain clearing. He lay back with an arm crooked beneath his head for a pillow. He drew at the tobacco and idly watched the scuttle creeping up the slimy pile. He must try to think.

So he'd been right: they'd brought him to the *San Marco*, the ship he'd been covering for so long. She was some sort of converted whaling ship, a giant, clumsy-looking vessel amongst the sleek ships around her, with her broad beam. This cell must be up in the port bow somewhere, for the ship was alongside and facing inshore. But why the devil should von Kramer be connected with her, and why, in heaven's name, should the stinker react so violently?

At least Hank had kept his head in the hotel: he'd managed to leave some clue for Peter, anyway. He had intended to tell him of Kramer's whereabouts; Hank had never dreamed he'd be incarcerated in the same ship. The chances were nil of Pete following up his message in the Bible; Hank had only enough time to underline the heading with his thumbnail. But there *was* a chance: he felt sure he had mentioned the ship in Joe Croxton's office.

So his thoughts whirled round until the sun came up and began climbing into the sky. The light brightened in his cell, and at six-thirty the door again opened. An officer stood in the doorway.

"Herr Jefferson, my orders are to see you are treated correctly," the man said. He was the typical Nazi type: hatchet-faced, a scar down his cheek and expressionless eyes. "You will come to no harm if you give no trouble. The Kommandant will see you after the tugs have turned the ship."

Hank grinned. "*Danke schön*," he said. "Very good of you, *mein Leutnant*. And when may I expect the honour of meeting His Excellency?"

The officer flushed. "We sail on the tide," he said. "At noon."

He stood aside. A sailor passed a tray through the doorway and Hank took it hungrily. The rolls and coffee looked good. At least they weren't starving him. The door slammed and Hank was left alone once more with his thoughts. He never felt more depressed. Four hours to go, and he'd be sailing, shanghaied, in this prison ship. Unless Pete could work some miracle, he was a dead duck.

Frozen, as motionless as a marble statue, Peter crouched in the shadow. Poised on the balls of his feet, ready to pounce, his eyes watched the wooden door open towards him. Inch by inch… He could smell the rot in the wood now; the door was flattening him against the wall, it was so close. He held his breath…

It all happened before he could think. A dark shape slipped through the gate. It was looking back over its shoulder, towards the street from which it had come. Then it loped up the garden path until it disappeared into the shadows beneath the house. It was so silent that Peter felt his flesh creeping. In a swift movement, Peter swivelled himself round the door. Then he was outside on the pavement.

The street lamps blinded him for an instant, the blue light under the plane trees weirdly dappling the stone flags. He glanced down the street in the direction of the back garden of the Günther Hof.

The street was deserted. He darted round the end of the wall which formed the junction with another side street leading to the main road.

He was in the shadows here. They'd still be watching the front of the crescent. If he moved into the main road they would pick him up at once. This block of flats on the opposite side of the road sealed off his escape.

He was surrounded, caught like a rat in those circular wire cages. The vermin can squeeze through but, once inside, cannot escape backwards. Panic was sweeping through him: he daren't remain here any longer.

Two cars were bearing down upon him, with sidelights burning. He was about to dash into the road to hail the leading car when some instinct checked him. He saw a red light glowing on the roof and, in German, *Police*, illuminated in bold letters. He melted into the shadows. If he threw himself on their mercy he would compromise the whole desperate business: better wait for the second car...

The next pair of lights was approaching so slowly that he thought the driver must be drunk. But then he saw the yellow light of a cab's meter. He slipped across the road and waited on the kerb. He must be visible now to anyone looking this way. His heart was banging against his ribs when he stepped forward in front of the taxi.

The driver leant forward and pulled the handbrake. He looked hard at Peter. He'd seen some queer things in Hamburg. He was fussy about his fares: for a moment Peter saw the suspicion in the man's eyes while he deliberated whether to drive on. Peter wrenched open the door and slumped back into the darkness of the back seat.

"Hauptbahnhof," he snapped.

He would be safe in the main railway station. He could lose himself in the crowds, even sleep there until dawn, for he had his return ticket to Flensburg. The driver leant across to reset the meter. The cab jerked, and the transmission whined as the vehicle resumed its journey. Peter lay back in the darkness. This was the critical moment. The cab was driving into the brilliance of the lights on the main road. If *they* stopped the taxi now...

He leant forwards and tapped the glass screen. "Quick as you can, *bitte*," he said. "I've a train to catch."

The driver must have assumed Peter was English. Middle-aged men of Hamburg find it difficult to forget the fire typhoon which raged in 1944. He'd show this young Englishman. He stabbed his foot on the accelerator as a figure loomed from the darkness and tried to cross his path.

Peter heard the guttural shouting. He saw the flash of a torch, caught the urgency in the stranger's voice. Peter slipped to the floor and crouched there, his head in the shadow and against the door. The beam of a flashlight suddenly spotlighted the black leather of the seat.

It was over in a second. The cabbie was swearing as he accelerated and pulled away from the stranger. Peter heard the guttural replies disappearing behind them and then the taxi was hurtling down the Tiergartenstrasse. He scrambled from his undignified position on the floor, dusted himself, and sat back grinning in the darkness.

That, at least, should finish it, he thought. *The swine won't remember the empty taxi.* But Peter was learning fast, learning to take no chances with this ruthless organisation. He tapped the window again and took the cab down the next turning on the right. And so, twisting and turning through the back streets of

Hamburg, the taxi finally reached the main railway station. Peter sighed with relief as he paid off the surly driver. The clock was glowing from the tower above him. It was one twenty-five in the morning. He *must* have time to think. So far he was lucky to have survived. He moved through the barrier, found the waiting room and stretched out on the only empty bench. He pulled his mac closer round him, festooned a paper over his face. The cold of the dawn would wake him. In a few minutes he was asleep.

Hank Jefferson lay back on his bunk. He dragged at the cigarette, his third. He would have to ration himself. Yet it was odd how the cell did not fug up. He blew out the smoke and idly watched it curling upwards. At least the cell was properly ventilated: she must be a modern ship, at any rate. From the little he had glimpsed of her, she was a bulbous brute, bristling with gantries and samson posts.

And the visit to the Kommandant? He was not looking forward to this. (Perhaps it wasn't Kramer.) If it was the same devil — and Hank's stomach slumped as he remembered the cruelty of the brute — at least one thing would be proved: they were on the right track.

He looked at his watch: eleven-ten. Time was slipping by; the tide would not wait. It was then that he heard the wire hawsers scraping across the deck above him. So they *were* preparing for sea?

He groaned as he realised the impossibility of his predicament. No one knew of his whereabouts; he was Kramer's prisoner; and within the hour he could easily be just another corpse floating down the Elbe and bumping against the piles in the port of Hamburg. He knew Kramer's technique by now: try the soft treatment first. But he, Hank Jefferson, wouldn't squeal…

He lay back on his bunk, listening to the preparations for sea; by kneeling on the mattress, he could just see through the thick, barred scuttle. There on the wharf, thirty feet below him, groups of stevedores were collecting.

He felt a bump and the ship swung towards the jetty. The tugs must be alongside. It was then that the shock hit him: the final realisation that he, Lieutenant Jefferson, D.S.C., U.S.N., was washed up, kaput… There was nothing that he could do. In less than an hour this lumbering whaling ship would be slipping down on the tide, away from his only hope of succour. The last phase of his short existence had begun already.

Already they had begun swinging *San Marco* across the basin: he could feel her thudding as she strained under the wires, and (look at the size of the thing!) they were slipping the fore spring…

He saw the bight of the 5½-inch wire splash into the water as the fo'c'sle party let go the spring. He watched the stevedores running away with the inshore end; saw the wire snaking from the basin to leave a greasy, snail-like trail across the jetty. The gap between the ship's port bow and the concrete wharf began to widen. He saw the scum floating between the piles, the filth of Hamburg, then the oily black water as the gap grew. The roof of the wharf came into view then, the cranes, the masts and derricks of ships on the other side. He tried to drag away his eyes as she swung in the basin: the tugs were turning her in her own length, so that she would be pointing downriver on the ebb. And, he had to hand it to them, they were showing their usual efficiency: *San Marco* was obliquely across the basin now, her bows swinging fast to starboard. If they weren't careful, she'd touch at this end: she was swinging rapidly towards the other side of the basin … he could look no longer. His knees ached in this cramped position. He didn't relish being against the side when she bumped.

He swung his legs over the side of the bunk. He lit another cigarette; he squinted inside the crumpled packet — only three left. In his misery he could not collect his thoughts.

Fine effort so far! His life about to be snuffed out, Peter probably a 'stiff' with a knife in his back, and all for what? God, he wished he knew. There were, at least, two definite facts.

He swung his legs to get the circulation moving; he took a long pull at the weed and blew out the blue smoke — disgusting habit this. He must give it up, or he'd be joining the other weak-minded brethren: on the operating slab, with a white-masked surgeon bending over him, scalpel poised over his chest. But it didn't matter now. Lung cancer had little meaning when he was about to be murdered anyway.

He gazed, mesmerised by the blue circles of the cloud, smoke rings curling upwards toward the exhaust outlet in the deckhead. Slowly they rose, curling and swirling into an ordinary ventilator grille. Because this was a tiny offender's cell, isolated in the fore-ends of the ship, perhaps it was not connected with the ship's main ventilation system. Probably merely a torpedo vent on the upper deck, with its head clear of the scuppers, or even tucked in under the flare of the ship's side.

Crazy how you worried about little things when larger issues loomed — his curiosity was aroused by this ventilation problem. If he blew out a large puff of smoke near the exhaust, he might be able to see it issuing along the side if, in fact, the torpedo vent was sited under the flare. He took a long pull at the cigarette, held the smoke in his mouth for a moment, then exhaled it under the exhaust inlet. He smiled ruefully to himself. *Ought to have been a perishing plumber*, he thought, as he climbed back to his bunk. By straining his neck he could see for'd several yards along the plating of the port bow.

He shut his right eye: ah! That was better. He grinned as he saw a wisp of blue smoke guff out of the side above his head. So his theory was correct: he'd apply for a transfer when he reached heaven or The Other Place.

His gaze wandered across the expanse of water. Another tug had tucked herself inside this port bow, and was waiting to be passed a heaving line. He could see the deckhand waiting patiently there, one foot on a coil of rope, a spare heaving line in his hand.

San Marco's bows were swinging fast now and were nearly at right angles to the jetty on the other side of the basin. He squinted downwards and could just see the wharf: it was a strange feeling, towering above this concrete, trapped in this steel cell and isolated from civilisation and safety. He could see a loafer lounging against the pillars supporting the wharf roof, a dockyard policeman watching yet another ship manoeuvring for the tide; a kaleidoscope of colour as a party of schoolchildren stopped to watch for a moment the Leviathan towering above them. He could see them suddenly cease their chatter, he was so close to them. Their mouths were hanging open; a little girl raised her hand and slowly waved, shyly at first, then with gusto as someone on the deck above him replied. The whole party broke into shouts, yelling and waving. Ah, well…

He was turning away, sickened by the tantalising sight, when he noticed a man standing in the shadows by one of the pillars. Afterwards, when he thought about it, he could not have said why this individual had caught his attention. Something alien in his manner of dress, perhaps. The face was invisible in the shadow, but, from the way he leant casually against the pillar, a chord suddenly vibrated in Hank's memory. Maybe it was because of his hypersensitive state; perhaps his senses were sharpened (as some men aver who have returned from the near-dead), but for whatever the reason, Hank's consciousness suddenly clicked into acute awareness. It was probably the grey flannel trousers and the brown leather brogues that only an Englishman dare wear...

Dammit, it was Peter! Peter was there, dear God! Hank was certain it was him, leaning against that pillar. So he'd picked up the clue. In Hank's anguish, he beat his fists against the plating of the ship's side. How could they contact each other now — how, for God's sake, could he let Peter know that he was within a few yards of him, but incarcerated in this accursed ship?

The bows had stopped swinging for a moment, so Hank could see better. Yes, it was Peter, he was certain. Hank waved his arm across the scuttle, beat on the bars: but it was useless. Peter's face was in darkness.

Hank was beside himself. He flung round swiftly, unable to bear it a moment longer. He took another pull at his cigarette...

The next sixty seconds moved very swiftly. Hank stared for an instant at his straw pillow. He snatched it and leaped down from his bunk. He struck a match and held it under one corner of the pillow. A few seconds and the straw was alight. He fanned it slowly to start the flames crackling, and then, when it was well alight, he smothered it on the bunk.

He coughed and spluttered as his lungs gasped for air. The cell was thick with brown smoke. He held up the smouldering pillow below the exhaust inlet. The thick smoke whooshed away, swirling into the ventilator trunking. The draught caused the pillow to flame again. He threw it on the deck and stamped it out. The smoke continued to billow upwards.

In order to breathe at all, he had to jump back on to the bunk. He could see a circle of daylight through the scuttle. He pressed his face against the thick glass — yes, there was Peter...

The man had half-turned towards the bows of the ship and was facing Hank. That was Peter Sinclair all right. Hank beat his fists against the bars until the blood ran from his knuckles.

Keep your head down, man, don't panic, for God's sake... Pete cannot possibly see me through this plate-glass scuttle: only six inches wide and against a dark background.

Hank tore the matchbox from his pocket. He struck a match, waited until it was flaming, then passed it slowly across the bars. He traversed the scuttle four times in quick succession. The flame was burning well now and flaring in the darkness of these thick fumes.

He snuffed out the flame between his finger and thumb. He struck another match, waited for it to flare, then quickly passed it across the scuttle. Now again, slowly, then once quickly; slowly again, then once quickly ... until the message was finished. Then he repeated the performance, his heart pounding in his eardrums, his lungs clamouring for air, until he was forced to jump back to the bunk.

The ship had swung past the halfway mark. Hank could still see Peter moving quickly along the wharf, in the shadows but keeping pace with the scuttle which would be soon shielded from his view by the ship's stern.

Keys were rattling in the door of his cell. He leapt from the bunk. He began throwing his arms about wildly; he was shouting for help, mouthing incoherently, and stamping on the smouldering remains of his pillow when the door opened.

The officer who came to take him was terrified too: an inferno was raging in here. Then Hank slumped to the deck, apparently unconscious. His eyelids were closed, but he felt better. Even now, as he felt these swine dragging him from the cell, he could not shut out the image in his mind.

Peter had been smiling. He had waved and stretched out his arms horizontally. His fingers had been stiff and rigid, and three times he did this: this was an R for Roger in semaphore. And R for Roger meant, *Message Received...*

.... .— —. —. —, ...— —. —. —

Peter had read the morse. Hank could do no more. He went limp and allowed them to lug him into the fore-peak.

CHAPTER 6

Loosed from the Traps

"Deputy Director of Naval Intelligence speaking."

Even from this distance, Peter recognised the soft but incisive voice of Joe Croxton. The 'scrambler' telephone line between the Commander-in-Chief's office, Hamburg, and Admiralty was classified as confidential, but was not secret. Peter could take no chances.

"Sinclair here, sir."

"Yes."

"They've got Hank."

"Ye-e-s," the soft voice said at the other end. "Go on."

"Request permission to act independently, sir. Emergency."

Peter heard the humming of the line, then a barely perceptible click somewhere along the circuit. Someone was tapping the line. He tensed, his mind racing.

"What d'you want me to do?" the Deputy Director asked.

"Give me full authority, sir, to act as I think fit. The Commander-in-Chief here may not like it."

"Dusty Miller will agree." Joe Croxton was chuckling at the other end. "I was his Third Hand in H.22."

"Can I go ahead, sir?"

"Go ahead, Sinclair. But keep me informed."

The phone went dead. The enemy can't have got much out of that. Peter buttoned up his reefer and moved through to the adjoining office.

"May I see the Admiral?" he asked the secretary.

Flags, a pleasant fellow wearing aiguillettes, ushered him through to the Holy of Holies. The Admiral, a rotund, red-faced man with sharp eyes indicated the chair. He was relighting his pipe when his personal phone shrilled on the desk.

"Damn," he muttered as the match burnt his finger. His bushy eyebrows lifted. "Yes? Yes, put me through." He glared across at the young lieutenant on the other side of the desk. "Joe? Dusty here."

There followed a series of humphs! and umms! Then he looked long at Peter from under his eyebrows.

"All right, Joe," he said. "For you, yes. You always were crazy." He slammed down the receiver.

He glared at Peter across his desk before coming to a decision.

"What d'you want, Sinclair?" he snapped. "It's the first time a lieutenant has *told* an Admiral what he's going to do."

"Second time, sir," Peter grinned. "Captain Croxton was the first."

The Admiral snorted. He scratched his ear.

"When was that?"

"Yalta, sir; during the war."

"Get on with it then. And don't let me in on any secrets, me lad. Might compromise them." The Admiral's eyes were dangerous.

"I'd like to put to sea immediately in *Rugged*, sir. May I be detached from the U.N.O. squadron to act independently, sir? I'll look after myself."

The Admiral snorted. "You know damn well my command is strained to the limit."

There was a long silence.

"D.N.I. believe this to be vital, sir," Peter said quietly. "I shouldn't ask unless it were a matter of life or death."

"Who for, boy?"

"A friend of mine, sir." Peter paused. Then he looked the Commander-in-Chief squarely in the eye. "He's under sentence of death," he added. "Kidnapped."

"You don't want an escort?"

"No thank you, sir. I'll look after myself."

The Admiral prised himself from his chair and showed Peter to the door.

"I'll take care of the signals," he said, taking Peter's hand. "Make a good job of this."

"A lot depends on it, sir."

"Promotion's bad these days."

Peter nodded. He was impatient to be gone. Every second counted now that the *San Marco* was steaming down the Elbe. She'd be in the North Sea in an hour or two.

"Anything else you want, Sinclair? I've brought *Rugged* to immediate notice for sea."

"Can you fly me up to Flensburg, sir?"

The Admiral grunted. He grabbed the second telephone on his desk. "Chief of Staff? Yes … bring my 'chopper' to immediate notice. Yes … to take Lieutenant Sinclair to Flensburg. He'll tell the pilot — yes, that's all."

How pleasant to be an Admiral, Peter thought, as he waited, still in plain clothes, for the Commander-in-Chief to dismiss him.

The Admiral opened the door. "Flags," he bellowed. "Tell my chauffeur to take this officer to the heliport."

Peter was already at the door. He stood to attention. "Thank you, sir."

"Get cracking, my boy," the Admiral shouted. "Good luck. You won't get a chance like this again."

Peter felt an arm across his shoulders. Then he was outside, trotting after the Flag Lieutenant.

After leaving Flensburg, *Rugged* steamed on a south-easterly course on the surface. She dived before altering round to the north-east. Peter wanted no prying eyes to witness his departure. When they had settled down at periscope depth, he sent for his First Lieutenant.

"Well done, Number One. Nice, smooth getaway."

"Bit of luck I hadn't given leave, sir."

"Any absentees?"

"No, sir. Able Seaman Hawkins nearly missed his ship."

"How?"

"'Rabbiting' in the dockyard."

Peter smiled. What the dickens was Hawkins up to now? The old rogue was always up to something. They'd shared so much together in the past that Peter could read his mind.

"More tiddly-bits for his store, I'll bet."

Benson nodded. "He's 'won' one or two Lugers, sir, I believe."

"Damn fool," Peter grunted. "He'll get me into trouble one of these days. I daren't ask what he swapped them for."

Benson was grinning and shaking his head.

"Well, how's the boat?" Peter asked as he climbed to his feet to change into his sea-going rig. "Shipshape and Bristol fashion?"

"Everything's fine, sir. Stored up for three months." Benson was grinning. "Never know where our skylarks will end up, sir."

"You're learning."

There was a knock on the door of the Captain's cabin and Lieutenant Ewan Craig, the Engineer Officer, stood in the doorway. He was in spotless white overalls and he carried a chromium torch in his hand. He was of medium build, and spoke with a soft, West Highland lilt, caressing every syllable. Peter could depend on the Chief: he was at his best in emergencies.

"Come in, Chief. Sit down. How's the plumbing?"

The Chief smiled and drew out the third chair from a corner of this minute but solidly furnished room. With the traditional mahogany furniture, the cretonne covers on the two armchairs, it was difficult to believe they were at one hundred feet and charging through the depths at eighteen knots. But with her Asdics and sonar built into her fore-ends, she could feel her way about in the dark. Though she was at immediate notice when on U.N.O. patrols, with six fish up the spout, her function in wartime was as a 'killer' submarine: to find, hunt and destroy enemy submarines.

"Reactor all right?" Peter asked.

"Fine, sir," the Chief replied. "Had a bit of trouble with number two distiller."

"All right now?"

"I'm keeping my fingers crossed, sir." The dour face wrinkled into the nearest approach to a smile of which Craig was capable. His blue eyes, the distant blue of the Western Islander, danced. It amused him when there were breakdowns in the conventional auxiliaries: the reactor gave no trouble. *It had better not this trip*, Peter thought. *I don't know how far we're going, but I want every knot I can get out of her for this first twenty-four hours.* He stood up and moved across to his small chart table.

"Come and have a look."

As he pored over the rock-studded chart, his mind was racing. How much did he dare tell his fellow officers? It was top secret, the whole incredible business. Yet he had to have the confidence of his officers. If anything happened to him, how would Benson know how to cope? He made up his mind. He'd tell them a limited amount — Kramer's kidnapping of Hank Jefferson; no more. Number One and the Chief knew him well enough to realise he would tell them all he could.

And so, tracing their D.R. through the restricted waters, he took them past Langeland, through the angry waters of the Store Baelt; he left Zeeland and Kalundborg to starboard.

"I'm surfacing at dusk, Chief," he said. "Concealment and best speed are the essentials at the moment."

"I wondered why we didn't use the Kiel canal," Benson murmured. "Too public."

Peter smiled as he looked up sideways from the chart: "You know, Number One, if you persist in showing this brilliance, I shall be forced to recommend you for your perisher. What'll I do for a Number One?"

Benson chuckled. "Pilot's itching for a Jimmy's job, sir. He'll do." He was stooping over the chart. "But I shouldn't worry: rarely do I have these flashes of genius."

Peter felt again the companionship of his officers around him. How lucky he was — *Rugged* was a fine 'nuclear', with a grand ship's company. It would be his fault, and his alone, if anything were to upset their happiness. He knew how miserable an unhappy boat could become.

His mind wandered over the fascinating problem of human relations as they traced their track over the chart. Up the Kattegat, round the Skan Lighthouse again, down the Skagerrak and into the North Sea, with Denmark fading into the distance on their port quarter.

"It's somewhere here that I hope to find *San Marco*." His finger traced a circle in the Straits of Dover. "I reckon she'll be steaming at cruising speed, about eighteen knots. She cleared the Elbe at about midnight and has a four-hour start on us — a lead of about three hundred miles. Let's see, it's the fifth of June, isn't it?"

He pricked off the distance on the chart and added four hours at eighteen knots: some three hundred and seventy-two miles.

"Let's say four hundred miles," he said. He laid off the *San Marco*'s course from Hamburg.

"She can choose 'down channel' or up the North Sea and around the Orkneys. What's your bet, Number One?"

Benson rubbed his chin. "Could she round North Cape, sir?"

"Unlikely. She doesn't appear to be mixed up with the Russians. My guess is she's making for the Atlantic and wants to be as unobtrusive as possible."

"She's a whaler, you say, sir?" The Chief had put down his torch and was engrossed by the crackling parchment of the chart. "Whalers go south."

"She certainly looked like one, or a factory ship of some sort. She had bluff bows, an enormous beam and dozens of cranes and derricks."

"Let's plump for the Channel then," Peter said. "Agree?"

"Why don't we ask Admiralty to shadow her? The R.A.F. or our birdmen could help."

"I daren't break W/T silence, Chief. Our codes have been broken: our security is non-existent. We must keep our intentions secret. I don't believe the enemy realise we know Jefferson's aboard the *San Marco*."

"Poor old Hank."

The remark escaped unconsciously from Benson. He liked the American commando; respected him for his courage and modesty. He'd certainly pulled the chestnuts out of the fire in the West Indies.

They were silent for a moment. Hank's life depended upon keeping tabs on the whaler.

"And if she were shadowed by aircraft," Peter continued, "she'd soon become suspicious. She's festooned with modern radar."

"As soon as she suspects she's being shadowed," the Chief added, "it's 'goodbye' for poor old Hank. She'll alter course and we'd never find her. In spite of our speed and radar, she would be like the proverbial needle in the haystack."

Peter's dividers spanned off the distances. "Overhauling at a relative speed of twelve knots," he mused, "we should be within her area about here. Don't forget she made about eighty miles before we even started."

"And twelve into four hundred's about..." Benson shut his eyes.

"Thirty-three hours," the Chief said.

"Cancel the 'perisher'," Peter added.

Benson grinned across the chart.

"And thirty-three hours at eighteen knots is...?" Peter looked hopefully at Number One.

"Five nine four miles," snapped the Chief.

Benson looked daggers, tilted back his head and laughed. "I'll stay as your Jimmy, sir."

"*Here*," Peter said quietly. "We should pick her up just about here." His finger was pointing to a position in the Straits of Dover.

"Between Beachy and Boulogne, that's where we'll find her, about dawn on Sunday, the sixth."

CHAPTER 7

First Meeting

By the time they finally unlocked the store into which they'd thrown him, Hank had reached a conclusion. If his adversary proved to be von Kramer, there was only one hope: human life was worthless — nothing was sacred to this brute of a man. *If Kramer hadn't wanted something out of me*, Hank argued with himself in the darkness of his new lockup, *then I should be floating face-down in the Elbe, with my throat cut. I sign my own death warrant as soon as I part with my side of the bargain. Now, what the devil does he want?*

He remained squatting on the sacks in the store, and blinked at the sudden light. Strong-armed men dragged him to his feet.

"Up, *schweinhund!*"

The man who delivered the swinging kick at Hank's groin was dressed in the ridiculous but sinister uniform of the old S.S.: black jacket, riding breeches and jackboots. On his head he wore an ostentatious black cap, with its cap badge, the foul insignia of which they were so proud: a silver death's head.

"Still playing at being Nazis?" Hank grinned, jerking free his body. His judo training sent one of his guards spinning along the steel deck. Hank ducked as the other guard grabbed him. Then up came Hank's left, his whole weight behind it. He felt the officer's nose give beneath his knuckles. He saw the blood welling as three toughs leaped on him from behind.

He felt the boot as it smashed into his ribs. There was a moment of excruciating pain; he lay on the deck, winded and clawing for breath while his muscles refused to act.

His world went black, spun around him, wavered and reeled until he felt sick. Yellow stars swam before his eyes, danced, then settled slowly into a swinging motion until they slowly disappeared. He dragged himself back from half-consciousness; he was jerked to his feet... He was being frogmarched down a passage. He shook his head and tried to memorise the route.

Impossible. The pain was spread throughout the lower part of his abdomen. As they took him into a lift, he felt his ribs. He breathed in and out slowly and gradually felt his wind returning. No ribs broken.

Then they were stepping out into a corridor. He felt the air of the sea blowing upon his face. He heard the squawk of a gull, and then he was swaying upon the upper deck of this lumbering vessel. As they hauled him along the deck, he could see the grey seas coming up to meet him; to disappear a moment later as the gunwales swung into the sky with the roll.

His guards were obviously not seamen. They staggered with their prisoner, lurching along the steel plating and crashing into the superstructure as they made their way aft.

Hank felt better as he watched the Nazi dodging clear of him. The brute kept a couple of paces ahead as he led the way to what must be the officers' quarters. Hank knew again the wind in his hair, felt his reeling senses returning, began to take in details as he was hustled aft.

They were on a catwalk now, stumbling down the port side of the ship. He could see no land, just the grey-green of a dull, cold sea. *Must be somewhere off Holland*, he thought, *visibility looks low over there. There's that typical yellow tinge, with the haze lying low on the horizon.* He glanced skywards. A pale brightness behind the low-flying cloud gave hint of the sun.

The ship's bows were ugly, like an old L.S.T.'s. They were pointing south-west. If he was right, they were bound down-Channel.

A dig in the small of the back reminded him that this was no promenade around the upper deck. They staggered in single file along the catwalk. Hank took his time. The more he assimilated his surroundings, the better chance he had. He looked down to his right.

She was an enormous whaling factory ship; no doubt about that. They were walking aft, and down below him was a great well, about the size of two tennis courts. Along the side were innumerable fittings: hose connections, small gantries, yes, and even an overhead travelling crane.

He had been incarcerated in the eyes of the ship. On his way back, he'd take a closer look. He was sure she had the bulbous bows of an enormous L.S.T., a great ramp which could open to admit the carcase of a whale. In fact, the ship was a seagoing floating dock, with powerful engines: she had a funnel on either quarter where the caisson-like sides joined the after-bulkhead of the vast well.

Hank followed the man down into the accommodation quarters. He could feel the guards breathing down his neck as they followed on his heels. These quarters were spacious: big enough for state rooms.

"Halt!"

The escort jerked to attention. Hank bumped deliberately into the next ahead.

"So sorry."

He grinned at the S.S. officer. The man ignored him, swept off his cap and knocked on the door. Over the lintel, in large German characters, was a tally: *Kommandant.*

Ah-ha! The Big White Chief…

Someone pushed him hard from behind when the door swung open. He found himself in an anteroom; it was spotlessly clean, the white paint gleaming under the lights. A jack-booted sailor was standing guard outside the further door. In the corner was a desk from which another S.S. character was rising.

"The Kommandant will see him now," the man said softly, as they exchanged the Nazi salute. The system was ingrained deeply into these men: the raised arm and the outstretched hand came naturally to them. As in the old days, the action was a greeting as much as a salute. Hank wondered who the Führer was now. Why did they carry on with this caper so openly? The whole ship must be Nazi...

The sentry opened the door. The secretary led the way into the inner sanctum. Hank followed. The thugs brought up the rear. In front of them stood a wide, empty desk. Hank heard the door closing behind him. He looked round quickly. There was an enormous man leaning against the bulkhead. He had one hand in the pocket of his breeches; the other toyed with a cigar.

Beneath the man's large, square forehead, two eyes glittered. They were bright and deep-sunk into the skull. Shrewd, intelligent, Hank had difficulty in holding those piercing eyes. The man was bald, though white stubble protruded above his ears, like the bristles on a boar. He must be in his sixties: he was huge, yet had no stomach on him. He looked what he was: a ruthless, tough and seasoned leader.

Hank grinned. The coincidence was too ridiculous.

"So, Herr..." The Kommandant scratched the side of his pate with a stubby finger (Hank heard the scraping of the bristles). "We meet again, *hein*?"

Hank nodded, but remained grinning. He was saying nothing. Let the big German do the running. The fellow was von Kramer all right, Ulrich von Kramer. No doubt about it now. Hank hadn't wrestled for his life with that German for nothing. You could never forget Kramer — he was the most terrifying individual Hank had ever met. Sinister, evil, yet giving the impression of immense power inside that gigantic figure. And controlling the whole mechanism, a shining skull with a pronounced cranium, inside which a brilliant brain functioned. The German moved silently towards him. Hank felt the skin prickling at the back of his neck.

Hank stood his ground, a Nazi officer at each elbow.

"You find this amusing, eh, *mein Herr*?"

The piggy eyes glittered, an inch from Hank's face. The American squared his shoulders and poised himself on the balls of his feet. His hands twitched. By a supreme effort at control, he did not lash out. A muscle in his cheek twitched.

"You all look so goddarned stoopid," Hank said quietly.

A movement like lightning, as swift as a rattlesnake striking, and Hank felt a blow stinging across his cheekbone. He tried to move, but felt his arms pinioned at his sides. He saw Kramer wiping the back of his hand with a handkerchief, a delicate light blue silk affair. Hank spat the blood from his mouth and saw the red stain darken the pile of the carpet at his feet. He was winning so far. Kramer had lost Round One by losing his temper: perhaps if Hank goaded him enough, he'd betray the purpose of his kidnapping.

"You filthy bit of work, Kramer."

But it was Kramer who was smiling now. "So you do not forget a face, *hein*? You remember it always, a face like mine, *hein*?"

Kramer allowed his face to relax. The structure became mobile and instantly the effect changed. No longer a ruthless, boorish Hun, the image was that of a dissolute businessman, slack-jowled, self-indulgent, sharp. Hank recalled how Peter had once said that Kramer was one of the most dangerous men in the world: he'd been one of Himmler's henchmen, though he'd run into trouble there, it was believed. Kramer had been one of Himmler's top agents, a master of intrigue and disguise, yet with a brilliant, organising mind. He'd not been O/C Security at the Citadel for nothing.

"A pity for you, Jefferson, that you recognised me. When I saw you in Hamburg, I wondered whether you'd noticed me, whether you'd remember me after these years. You realise, of course, I was supposed to have died at Nuremberg?" There was a hint of pride in his voice.

Hank looked surprised as Kramer continued: "Yes, my friend. Until *you* ran across me the other day, there was no one on your side of the fence," (his eyes were pinpoints of light), "no one in the world who could have identified me. And now from you, you idiot, there's only one thing I want to know."

The American looked disinterested. He was preoccupied with cleaning up the broken skin at the corner of his mouth.

"Damn you, you American swine, answer my question."

Hank looked up, straight into the eyes of the German. "Which is?"

Kramer hesitated. He moved across the state room and sat down behind the desk. He seemed worried by his lack of control.

"Listen carefully, Jefferson," he said, trimming his nails with a pair of nail clippers. The instrument flashed under the glare of the lights. Hank was again amazed by the sudden shift in the man's personality.

"Yeah?" Hank drawled.

The German slowly raised his head. He gazed at Hank from under his bushy eyebrows.

"Did you recognise me, Jefferson? Did you remember me? For fifteen years no one has recognised me…" he was saying softly. "Did you tell anyone of your suspicions, Yank?"

Hank's whole being was alert now. His instinct was flashing danger signals to his brain. This was the moment, this the instant of truth. He felt Kramer's eyes boring into his, searching, prising deeply for the truth. The sixty-four-thousand-dollar question…

Hank smiled, playing for time while his mind raced. If he bluffed, Kramer might guess the lie. If he told the truth, that would be the end of the matter: Kramer would know the worst, redeploy his forces. Once Kramer had the facts, Hank Jefferson was dead.

"Have you told anyone, Jefferson?"

Kramer's eyes were still boring through him. There was now an edge to his question. Hank smiled down at him. If he 'acted wet' long enough, Kramer might give away his own *raison d'être*.

"What the hell's that got to do with you, bud?"

The Americanism stung the Kommandant to the quick. He was not used to insolence, Hank could see that. Now the swine was climbing to his jack-booted feet again. He returned from the desk and stood close to his prisoner.

"Much depends upon your answers to my two questions, Yank," he said silkily. "Your life and perhaps the lives of many others." His eyes were glinting. Hank had never seen such an evil, savage face. "Yes, many others, Jefferson," Kramer mused. "But we have a little time yet, my friend. I give you until noon tomorrow for an answer."

Hank stuck out his chin aggressively. "Suppose I won't talk?"

The German came close and spat in his face. Hank tried to move his head, but the spittle smeared down his cheek. His guards tightened their grip.

"You *will* talk, Jefferson, you will. My technique has changed a good deal since we last met. You see, my good friends, the Russian G.R.U., recently taught me a thing or two. You'll talk. Just you see, you'll talk…"

The German was lighting another stubby cigar. He blew the smoke into Hank's eyes. "If you prove to be my first failure, my American friend, I'll go on until you die."

He turned to the senior of the two S.S. men.

"Take him away."

CHAPTER 8

Down Channel

Friday dawned clear. It was one of those brassy, metallic dawns, with visibility over twenty miles; a bad sign, with rain certain to follow. From *Rugged*'s fin, Peter watched the steely streak of first light breaking astern of them. He lowered his binoculars and turned to the Officer of the Watch, Sub-Lieutenant Ian Taggart, the Navigating Officer.

"We're in luck, Pilot — maximum visibility. Keep your eyes skinned right ahead."

Peter felt the wind blowing through his hair. With her twenty-eight knots on the surface, *Rugged* must be overhauling rapidly. He'd switched off the surface-scanner: he dared not risk rousing the suspicions of the *San Marco*. There was so much shipping in the Channel that each 'blip' on the scan was unsettling. Even if *Rugged* missed her enemy, at least she would pass ahead and could lie in wait down-Channel. But once dived, the task of identification and interception was more difficult, even with an underwater speed of thirty knots.

They had investigated, undetected, every ship they had passed down the Dutch coast. With her navigation lights extinguished, the black silhouette of the submarine, trimmed well down, was invisible as she slipped towards The Downs. No one expects a darkened ship in peacetime, least of all a submarine which is so vulnerable to collision.

Peter looked over the stern at the bubbling, threshing wake. It showed, a white ribbon, a finger pointing along the track from which they had come. But already the silver streak in the sky to the eastward had changed to grey, and low down, along the horizon line, the duck-egg green of twilight painted the dawn sky. Then, minute by minute the waking sun, still yawning below the skyline, crept from the horizon to wash the sky the palest of pastel pinks, greens and lemon-yellows.

He could still see the *Goodwin* lightship flashing its warning, far out on the starboard quarter. Abeam to starboard the South Foreland was coming up, its light blinking in short groups of three flashes every twenty seconds; ahead clustered innumerable white stern lights of ships they were overtaking. To starboard, two green bow lights and the steaming lights of a couple of ships passing up-channel. She must be a passenger liner by the look of her: a mass of twinkling lights, lines of glow-worms in the darkness, tier upon tier.

These dawns still thrilled Peter. He sniffed the air for the land smells, heard the swish of the seas swirling along her pressure hull. He savoured every moment, because any minute now he would be forced by the dawn to dive. *San Marco*, he reckoned, would pass through the centre of the Dover Straits and leave the Varne to port. To be unobtrusive, she'd have to proceed down the centre of the channel, leaving the Bassurelle Bank to port also. There was Cap Gris-Nez now, flashing its urgent warning, where once the Germans mounted their big guns. He lifted his binoculars to identify the light.

He could hear the lookouts handing over, heard Goddard, the Signalman, taking over his trick: he liked the 'morning' because it was the diving watch. He felt the Officer of the Watch moving round the bridge: these were familiar sounds, the very breath of their life, motivated by routine. This was seagoing, this was why he'd—

"There she is, sir! Red five…"

Taggart was shouting above the wind. Peter moved to the for'd end of the bridge. He clamped the binoculars to his eyes, gazed along the bearing, sweeping slowly from starboard to port — then back again until he found her ... ah, there she was, a smudge on the horizon line. He could just pick out her bulk. Yes, that *could* be her ... she was kicking up enough wake at her stern.

"Clear the bridge. Dive, dive, dive!"

He heard the vents opening, the water spurting upwards. He saw the lookouts tumbling through the upper lid and down into the darkness below. He swung into space. His feet dangled for the rungs of the ladder, his right hand-hauled down the upper lid and relief flooded through him. *San Marco* was ahead, and they were in contact. And, thanks be to God, for Hank's sake the ship could have no suspicion of being followed: *Rugged*'s radar monitor had picked up no transmissions.

It was suddenly very quiet. No sound now save the whine of motors and orders snapping from the Control Room. He slid out of the twill trunking and dropped into the light.

"Eighty feet; set sonar watch."

He would have to stay deep until after twilight. Blind at periscope depth would be suicidal in these waters, slap in the middle of the shipping lanes. He remained in the Control Room until Number One had settled her at the ordered depth.

"Watch Diving, Number One. Come to my cabin when you're ready. Pilot, keep the plot going."

The men stood back to allow their captain to pass down the narrow passage to the ladder which led up to his cabin. It was good to have so many of his old ship's company with him, comforting to know that, in spite of so many reverses, he could count on the loyalty of men like Able Seaman Hawkins. That man wielded a strong influence on the crew. The most experienced seaman on board, he had been with the Captain for more patrols than either of them could remember. When Hawkins was chasing Germans he was happy. Even today, the wounds had not healed: the loss of his wife, his little son and daughter in that nightmare air raid was something he could never forget.

As Peter swung up the short ladder he caught Hawkins's eye. A look of understanding passed between them; they'd shared much together, and just now Peter needed all the silent support his company could give him.

Peter knew that all was not well in the boat. Some of the younger hands were grumbling, the Coxswain had said. A new man, Leading Seaman Bloom, was causing trouble: he'd led a riot in Kiel and behaved stupidly. Now he was like a festering sore. Peter had been forced to punish him, and Bloom was resenting it. A disrated man should never have to live in the same messdeck, but, with that pierhead jump, Peter had been forced to take him with them.

Peter slumped down into the easy chair in his small cabin. He was tired, played out by the strain of the last forty-eight hours. Now, on top of the worry over Hank, he had to be given this niggling worry about Bloom. Dammit, couldn't the man realise that he, Peter Sinclair, was just as frustrated with events as he was? These months of inactivity, away from base, were bad for morale, and for too long now *Rugged* had been rotting out her guts. The trouble with Bloom was his young wife. She was the cause of his discontent. Bloom was doing all he could to get himself flung out of the boat, even to spreading sedition about his captain.

Peter sighed. A captain's life was a rotten one: lonely and nerve-racking. He'd had bad luck lately. That minor collision with the tug in the Clyde had not helped. Some of the younger

C.O.s were getting their first Mark IIIs already, those beautiful new 'nuclears' which were even smaller than *Rugged*. If Peter did not watch it, he'd be missing his promotion. He'd sensed this when he'd had that interview with Joe Croxton. His old C.O. had hinted that that was why he had been given this rotten job: a last chance for the promotion stakes. Competition was too fierce these days: the only operational commands were those in the U.N.O. Naval Security Force.

"Damn!"

Peter cursed beneath his breath. Now there was this inquiry hanging over his head. His accusations to higher authority over the deliberate ramming in the Baltic had brought swift response. A Board of Inquiry would be convening in Kiel on July 4th. The Germans would have his skin if they could; yes, even his own friends would find it difficult to support him at this moment, when Anglo-German unity in the U.N.O. alliance was so precarious. They'd refute his accusations; so would the Russians, the other mysterious partners in this unholy alliance: strange bedfellows in this U.N.O. Security Force. Peter smiled grimly to himself.

Even Admiralty would be forced to ignore his accusations. How could they support him if they could not disclose the vital mission upon which *Rugged* was engaged? Only Joe Croxton and a handful of secret agents even suspected the existence of such a plot. Their lips were sealed for their own safety and the secrecy of the counter-intelligence.

Peter's only chance was to bust this plot wide open. To try to save his friend's life was the first job. He must save Hank; the rest of the complications could go hang. If Hank was still alive, he must be aboard that whaling ship, the *San Marco*, steaming down-Channel two miles ahead of them.

Peter must hang on, like a puppy with a stick. All his skill would be needed to shadow successfully. If *San Marco* gave him the slip, it would mean the death of Hank, he knew that. Peter groaned within himself. Hank was probably over the side by now, if Kramer had no further use for him. The American wouldn't talk; Peter knew that from their experiences in the West Indies.

Peter glanced at his pipes in the pipe-rack. (He'd given it up for seven months now, but he still craved for a smoke.) There was one hope for Hank: perhaps Kramer was holding him as a hostage? There was one thing that swine did not know: had his organisation been reported? And if it had, how much did the Englishmen know?

Peter grinned, von Kramer was taking no chances if he was ruthless enough to order the sinking of a submarine in order to kill its commander. Whatever happened, Peter *must* hang on to this merchant ship. She was his only link with Kramer, his only link with Hank.

There was a tap on the lintel of his doorway. "Come in, Number One."

Peter looked up at his First Lieutenant. Benson, too, had come a long way with him. A grand chap: as trustworthy, as competent and loyal a First Lieutenant as one could find.

Peter stretched out a hand. "Sit down. All well?"

"Yes, sir. She's fine." The First Lieutenant smiled. "There's nothing to do in these nuclears."

"Can the sonar still pick up *San Marco* above our water noises?"

"Just, sir. No bother so far."

Peter grunted. Shadowing at eighteen knots below the surface was a novel experience. "If she gives us the slip, Jefferson'll lose his life. We're his only chance."

Benson rubbed the side of his nose with his finger. "If visibility stays like this, sir, we'll be all right. But in the middle of a shipping lane, life becomes confused. It's easy to start tracking the wrong ship."

"Thank God she's diesel."

"Helps, sir. But I'm worried."

"Cheer up, Number One. I'll surface at night, provided she remains unsuspicious."

Benson looked across at him, a query in his eyes. "You'll excuse me mentioning it, sir, but I think the troops would like to hear from you; they're a bit in the dark."

Peter nodded. Benson was a tactful First Lieutenant.

"I'm in the dark myself. But I'll talk to them when we come up for a look."

Number One had got up from his chair. "I must get below sir. I thought you ought to know about the troops."

"Thank you."

Peter watched Benson stooping to avoid the lintel. Strange how quickly life changed. Peter felt unsettled now that there was serious criticism amongst the crew. Still, you became used to loneliness at the top. What more could he tell them? Jeopardise the security of this wild goose chase? He'd have to tell them they were shadowing; but why, why in heaven's name should a nuclear be trailing a whaling ship?

He'd tell them the truth, not wrap it up. He picked up the mike. "All-round sonar sweep," he ordered. "Stand by for change of depth."

He picked up his cap, squared himself off in front of the mirror (was that grey face really his?) and climbed down to the Control Room. He glanced over the instruments on the panel. All well.

"Target's H.E., right ahead," Elliott reported. "Nothing else, sir."

Peter moved to the centre of the Control Room. "Periscope depth."

The First Lieutenant, standing squarely between the gauges, flipped the pump-order instrument. The mauve indicators flickered. He felt her tremble imperceptibly and then the bow-up angle coming on her. A quick look, a rapid fix if land was in sight, then down to eighty feet again. You couldn't use the periscope at eighteen knots: the flurry of spume would be picked up miles away.

"Stop motor."

The trembling faded, and suddenly all was quiet. This was a dangerous moment, these blind seconds between deep and periscope depth. This was the instant when a submarine could be ripped open in collision.

"Forty feet, sir," said the First Lieutenant, over his shoulder.

"Up periscope."

Peter pressed his forehead into the rubber facepiece: it was lighter now, a blue-green, limpid water. A white flurry, a smeary circle and suddenly his circle of vision jumped into focus.

There she was, right ahead. His heart raced. Hank *must* still be aboard that lumbering ship. Right ahead, her bulbous stern standing high, a white scar at her quarters as she ploughed westwards.

Peter swept round the horizon in low power: a tanker pushing up-Channel away to the northward, a plume of smoke trailing from her funnel. White horses; fleecy cloudlets stretching to the horizon — and, yes, there it was, bearing THAT, the pale whiteness of Beachy Head breaking chalkily through the haze of early dawn.

Strange how he had not sighted the *Royal Sovereign* lightship: must have missed her in this low visibility. In the Channel, June was notorious for fog. This visibility always recalled for him the agonies of war, the exhaustion and strain of running the bi-weekly convoys up and down the Channel.

"Green eight-o, sir."

"Down periscope. Ship's head?"

The helmsman grunted from his wheel at the for'd bulkhead: "Two-six-o, sir."

"I'm one hundred and sixty degrees on her starboard bow."

So the *San Marco* had altered course to the northward, had she? Interesting. Better have another look. He'd get a radar range before going deep again. A good fix was essential in these wreck-infested waters: he hated this speed with less than fifty feet of water below his keel. He flicked his fingers. The shining steel periscope slid upwards.

He grabbed the handles and peered once more into the binocular lenses: the momentary check as the glass cleared, the sudden leap into focus. The quick all-round look; then the methodical search along the sonar bearing.

"Bearing THAT, *San Marco*. Bearing THAT, Beachy. Take a radar range and bearing."

She stood up like a house now, a squat ugly ship. Her upper works were white, her hull grey — difficult to pick out in these misty conditions. Her twin funnels were right aft, one on either side, and wisps of diesel exhaust trailed from each.

As he watched, the bearing began drawing ahead. *Rugged* was well clear on the whaler's port quarter, but he dared not let her slip away.

He slammed shut the handles of the periscope. There was a hiss and the eighty-thousand-pound tube glided silently downwards.

"Eighty feet," he ordered.

He watched the pointers swinging slowly round the depth gauges as Number One took her down.

"Eighteen knots, Number One. Shadow *San Marco*, bearing Green seven-two."

"Aye, aye, sir."

Peter took the microphone from its bracket. He snapped on the switch. The speakers crackled in each compartment as he blew across the diaphragm.

"This is the Captain speaking," he began. "I thought you'd like to know what's up…"

He felt grim. In his mind he could see Bloom, face upturned and supercilious as he faced the loudspeakers in the fore-ends.

The familiar landmarks fell away astern. St. Catherine's, that notorious southerly headland on the Isle of Wight, came up just before dinner. Peter came to periscope depth hourly for a look, but only once was he in doubt of *San Marco*'s bearing. She was steady at about four miles; the only difficulty came a few minutes before dinner, when the Southampton-Boulogne ferry tore across and between them at the same moment as a Shell tanker swept up-Channel.

The island appeared, then slid astern, the teeth of The Needles looming briefly, white and ephemeral in the pale noonday.

St. Albans, that familiar headland which, in a sailing boat, was so difficult to make to windward in a westerly; then, when the hands had their heads down after dinner, the bluff of Portland. A strange shape — sinister and remote, the Bill always seemed to Peter. It was like a tensed beast, crouched to spring. He'd been caught on the edge of The Race once: that was enough. Ah! There was the lighthouse, a finger pointing skywards, yet, in reality, one hundred and forty-one feet high.

Across West Bay, that dangerous crescent, with its northerly set a menace to the small boat. Nothing to fix on, no identifiable landmarks in bad visibility. Berry Head, with its strange tower, came up after tea; the Pompey convoys used to make it their landfall when toiling for Dartmouth.

Past Start Point, sloping down so deceptively to the sea. The coast, rugged now, with Drake's Land, red-cliffed and white-necklaced, skirting the breaking seas. Eddystone, its sentinel, slipped away to starboard when the hands went to supper. And then, as twilight began to shut down, The Lizard, with its flat country behind. The Manacles, breaking white, a tumbling mass of foam; Coverack, once-upon-a-time a little, whitewashed, lobster-fishing village, but now a mecca for the charabancs.

But still the throb of *San Marco*'s screws plugging into the seas, pounding her way down the English Channel. Their steady beat had become part of their lives now, drum-drumming in Elliott's ears.

It was dark when Peter finally surfaced *Rugged*. He caught the loom of Land's End light, flashing to the northward. Ahead he could see *San Marco*'s stern light, bright in the darkness. He crouched over the voicepipe:

"Half-buoyancy," he ordered. "Lookouts on the bridge." He turned to the Officer of the Watch by his side.

"It's 0015, Pilot," he said to Ian Taggart, "and Land's End is giving us a good departure. D'you know what day it is?"

"Sixth of June, sir."

"Well?"

"Of course — D-Day, sir. Normandy landings."

"Soon forget, don't we?"

Peter turned away and felt the breeze blowing through his hair. The sixth of June, 1944. What memories that date brought to thousands of men — this lull before dawn, fear gripping their vitals as they wallowed across the Channel, their little landing craft butting through the seas towards the beaches: those strips of sand on which so many were to die before the sun had climbed above this morning's horizon.

"Don't get any closer, but keep her in sight, Pilot." He could hear the clattering of the lookouts as they took up their positions in the wings of the bridge. "Neither of us dare use radar because of 'D/effing'. Keep your eyes skinned. It's like the old days — the quick and the dead. Watch out for other shipping," Peter said quietly. "Trimmed down like this, we're invisible."

"Aye, aye, sir. What shall I do if she stops? I mustn't over-run her, must I?"

"Not if we want to rescue Hank Jefferson alive. His life depends upon our concealment." Peter instinctively lowered his voice. "Once they suspect they're detected, that'll be the end of Hank."

CHAPTER 9

Mortal Combat

"Captain in the Control Room!"

Peter's heart leapt into his mouth as he dragged himself past the Ward Room table to send the breakfast crockery rattling. O'Riley, the Ward Room flunkey, reeled backwards to avoid spilling the coffee he was carrying.

"Blimey," he muttered. "Same old routine." He shook his head and disappeared back down the passage. "Diving stations next."

"Diving stations!"

The submariners' call to action rang through the boat. Men poured from their bunks, flung themselves to the deck to stagger to their diving stations. In the Control Room the Captain was crouched low over the attack periscope. At the Plot, Taggart was recording the sequence of events.

"0702/7th June," he was writing in the log. "Sighted unidentified destroyer and one sonar helicopter, bearing 320°, stopped. Visibility 1 mile. *San Marco* H.E. fading on 340°." He jerked round to read the ship's head, and the relative bearing of the submarine. "Course 360°," he scribbled. "Speed reduced to 1½ knots to avoid detection."

He sprawled across the chart to mark their position: they'd come nearly a thousand miles since their departure from Land's End. They'd left St. Mary's, that peaceful little capital of the Scillies, twenty-five miles to starboard, and had maintained a steady course and speed until reaching their present D.R. position eighty-five miles due north of Flores in the Azores.

"Bearing THAT," the Captain was reporting in flat tones, his voice calm and controlled. "Destroyer, range THAT. Appears to be stopped. Helicopter hovering. Can't see *San Marco* now. Down periscope." He slammed shut the handles, watched the steel tube sliding down into its well.

"All-round listening watch on sonar," he ordered. "I can't make it out." He was scratching the side of his head and rubbing the side of his nose in those characteristic gestures of his. "That 'chopper' could be a sonar job, Number One. What the devil's going on? They seem to be some sort of A/S screen, covering *San Marco*'s alteration of course." He slapped his thigh in exasperation. "I daren't speed up, Number One, or they'll pick us up. Meanwhile *San Marco*'s disappearing to the northward." He turned towards his Navigating Officer. "What's her exact course, Pilot?"

But before Taggart could reply, Elliott, the black-haired H.S.D., was reporting from the sonar cabinet: "Asdic impulses bearing, Red four-o, sir. In contact. Slow destroyer H.E., Red eight-o."

His words ran like quicksilver through the boat. Some strange enemy was expecting them. It was inconceivable that this destroyer had blundered by chance into *Rugged*, a pinpoint in the ocean. This was deliberate. Their enemy's objective was to ensure *San Marco*'s undetected alteration of course. Peter glanced at the depth gauge: thirty-seven feet. He flicked his fingers; the attack periscope slid from its well. He knelt on the corticene to avoid showing too much 'stick'.

"Put me on Red four-o…"

George Hicks, the sandy-haired Stoker Petty Officer, spread his huge arms behind his Captain's shoulders. He eased the periscope round to the correct bearing and held it there.

"*On*, sir."

Daylight flooded suddenly into Peter's circle of vision. The water was running off the glass now, the lens smeary; then the image jumped into focus. The wavelets were slapping at the lens from the surface that ran away from him into the distance; an undulating swell, mauve and grey-streaked, merging into the heat haze.

"Can't see any—"

He tensed suddenly. He twisted the left-hand periscope handle.

"Bearing THAT."

The handles slammed shut. He'd seen enough. The steel tube streaked downwards.

"One hundred feet," he snapped. "Shut off from depth-charge attack."

He glanced at his watch: 0850. Then he turned slowly towards his First Lieutenant.

"This is a crazy situation, Number One. I daren't risk anything yet, though there's a helicopter on that bearing. I could see her sonar buoy hoist wire trailing in the water. The destroyer must be listening. If she's hostile, she may well run in and drop a pattern. I'm taking no chances."

"What then, sir?" Benson asked quietly. "They can stay here for ever, baulking our chase after *San Marco*."

Peter Sinclair looked his First Lieutenant squarely in the eye: "Stand by all tubes," he ordered, ignoring the question. "But I *must* wait for the swine to fire the first shot."

The deck was levelling off beneath his feet, when he heard Elliott reporting from the sonar cabinet: "H.E. increasing, Red eight-five. Sounds like steam-turbine, sir."

"She's a destroyer," Peter snapped. "Port fifteen."

"Boat shut off from depth-charge attack, sir. One hundred feet."

Peter nodded. He was watching the for'd watertight door swinging shut upon their world, a compartment twenty-five feet long by eighteen feet beam. They were restricted to this steel coffin now, their world bounded by these curved frames; every man aboard was now trapped in his own compartment. Conversation fell away as men spoke only in low voices.

Peter was watching the ship's head ticking round the compass tape. He took off the wheel ten degrees before the destroyer bore right ahead.

"Increasing speed, sir. Asdic transmissions, Green five-o."

"She's running in, Number One," said the Captain. "The chopper's sonar has got us taped. Open main vents."

He heard the thunk of the mushroom-shaped valves springing open. If *Rugged* was blown upwards by the explosions, no air could now become trapped in her main ballast tanks.

Peter glanced at his men. Grouped stiffly around the Control Room, they waited in silence, their bodies taut. The Coxswain did not take his eyes from the bubble of his inclinometer. A fine man, Peter thought, the backbone of the boat. With his greying hair and serene face, Chief Petty Officer George Withers, D.S.M., Submarine Coxswain, was 'father' to the ship's company. To him the youngest Ordinary Seaman took his troubles, his fears. Imperturbable, serene with the gentleness that comes only to those of a quiet mind, Withers had been through more emergencies than any man in the boat.

On his right, the Second Coxswain; black-bearded, flashy-eyed, tall and lanky, with tattoo marks wreathing round his arms and back, this was Petty Officer Jack Weston, the Don Juan of the boat. But now, thoughts of his shore conquests were pushed far from his mind. He was waiting, tensed and expectant, for the crack that would tear the 'planes from his hands and send the boat spinning downwards out of control...

Joe Saunders also, the Outside E.R.A., standing too nonchalantly by the panel, his arm outstretched along the main telemotor line. A Cornishman, with gingery hair, strongly built but quick in his movements, his was a vital job, requiring split-second timing.

Peter's eyes swept round to the for'd corner where George Hicks stood, the Stoker Petty Officer who read off the bearings and operated the periscope levers. He was standing with one foot on a valve box, his arms cradled across a bunch of valve spindles. He was staring upwards, his flaxen head cocked on one side, listening... He too could hear the transmissions.

Peter had hoped that only the experienced men would recognise this spine-chilling noise, this tick-ticking of the Asdic impulses bouncing against the pressure hull. Peter swore beneath his breath — there was no getting away from this sonar buoy dangling from the helicopter. He wished now that he'd found a temperature gradient at the beginning of the day; he could have dodged the impulses then...

Tick-tick ... tick-tick-tick ... there they go, all around you; faint tickings like the noise your finger and thumb make when you brush them together...

"Pass by phone to the motor room, 'Stand by for a burst of Emergency Ahead'," Peter snapped, nodding at Leslie Thatcher, the young Ordinary Seaman on the telephone. (If this swine 'up top' dropped a load, then *Rugged* was justified in retaliation. To sink the hunter seemed the only way out of their dilemma. And the helicopter? It could darn well run out of fuel and ditch. Why the devil this unholy partnership was centred eighty miles north of Fayal was a problem he'd have to solve later.)

"Transmission interval decreasing, sir. Range five hundred yards. All-round H.E."

Peter caught the H.S.D.'s eye as the man swept the headset from his ears: burst eardrums were unpleasant. In fact, Elliott had suffered this once before... Elliott, Peter noted, showed fear in his eyes. Peter's stomach sank. He'd never seen Elliott frightened before.

You could hear their hunter now: a crescendo of water noises and beating propellers. Pounding, pounding rhythmically, remorselessly above the bedlam as she thundered towards them. Then she was overhead, her cacophony swamping them.

"Emergency ahead!" Peter shouted, nodding at Thatcher. "Port twenty, steer one-three-o."

He waited, tensed on the balls of his feet, for the tremble when *Rugged* surged to full power. God, the motor room crew were slow ... would they never get her moving? Scared of blowing main motor fuses, probably... He glanced upwards when he heard the first patterns slapping the surface of the sea above them.

Faint slaps! that was all, as the patterns plopped into the sea ... in a second he'd catch the *snick!* of the strikers in the primers springing home. Ah! There they were. Even through this holocaust he could recognise this sound he dreaded above all others.

The charges were falling downwards through the water now, toppling, wobbling, straightening themselves out to strike end-on upon their pressure hull. God, would *Rugged* never move? He saw the knuckles of his fist growing white as he gripped the rungs of the ladder...

Then he felt it, a gradual trembling from the after-ends ... then a violent jerk — men stumbled where they stood as *Rugged* lunged forwards under full power.

Peter's eyes flicked to the pitometer log: two knots, five, ten, seventeen ... he held his breath: she was like a greyhound, loosed from the traps.

"Take that dive off the fore-planes," Benson yelled at the Second Coxswain. Peter felt the boat starting to plunge, her bows dropping beneath his feet.

"More rise on the after-planes," the First Lieutenant ordered the Coxswain. "Watch it, Coxswain, now ... don't let her porpoise..."

Peter watched the trimming team wrestling for control. It was like driving a B.R.M. in another element... She was moving now: thirty-two knots.

He did not know what happened next. There was an overwhelming roar, a crack that split their world apart. The frames jumped, the curvature of the hull springing like a concertina towards him. Involuntarily he jerked out his hands to ward off the blow ... he heard men gasping as the wind was sucked from their lungs. The curvature whipped back again. There were two more cracks, louder even than the first and once again *Rugged* was squeezed in a giant's fist.

Peter heard the catch in his breath, felt the pressure on his eardrums. He staggered against the ladder; he grabbed the rungs as the deck fell away beneath him. He watched the Coxswain toppling from his stool at the after-planes; he saw the First Lieutenant hurled against the Second Coxswain, knocking him from his seat. There was a shattering, sledgehammer shock — the lights flickered ... dimmed ... then flickered out as the deck fell away beneath their feet...

Then the rumble was overhead; there was a pounding as the destroyer began to fade across the starboard quarter, then the tinkling and chuckling of water noises. In the darkness, Peter knew that the bow-down angle was acute and growing steeper. He must stop this or it would be over before they knew it. Plunging out of control at this speed into these depths was suicidal: they'd be crushed to pulp in a few seconds, when the black waters engulfed them to squeeze them in their remorseless embrace...

"Stop motor! Get the secondary—"

The order remained unspoken on Peter's lips. The secondary lighting blinked on automatically to cast a baleful light on the shambles that was once the Control Room. Peter's eyes darted to the gauges.

Two hundred feet, the bubbles in the inclinometers hard up against the stops, no one on the T-handles of the planes. No wonder the boat was hurtling downwards out of control.

"Get back on the planes!" he shouted. He waited impotently while Benson tried to haul himself up the corticene deck, greasy now from the spilled slops, and sloping at a bow-down angle of forty degrees.

Peter nodded at the Outside E.R.A.: "Shut main vents. Blow one main ballast."

If the H.P. airline was intact, this should pull her out, but would Saunders be able to haul himself back to the panel in time? And *was* the line intact, not fractured by the shock? If the line was a 'gonner'...

Peter shut his eyes. This was the end, an abrupt termination to his life about which, in his nightmares, he had dreamed so often. The disintegration of the boat; the first creakings of the steel frames, the first tricklings of water seeping through the glands. Then the steady stream of water, the first faint suspicions of chlorine gas wreathing upwards through the battery boards beneath their feet. The twisting and crumpling metal next, the shudderings as the first compartments began to collapse; might even be the Control Room first — and he lifted his eyes upwards. The onrush of water as the hull crumpled, the screaming and writhing of metal, the men—

He shoved the horror from his mind. What the devil was he playing at? He *must* fight back. There was no future in passively waiting for the end. He, surely, was as capable of reaching the planes as anyone else? He began scrambling upwards, clawing at the periscope hoist wires to haul himself up the slippery slope.

Then, above the bangings and crashings of shifting gear, he heard it. He caught the sound, the glorious, familiar note of H.P. air screaming along the pipes. In a second he would know. Had the vents shut properly? Would the air reach number one main ballast tank? Four hundred and twenty feet on the gauges. Still the needle was swinging downwards, until it banged drunkenly against the stops…

Whee-eee…

From far away, from another world, distantly echoing from the fore-ends came the *thunk* of the main vent shutting. He held his breath. Only the air now…

Then, gradually, he felt it. It came as a gentle trembling at first, an imaginary shuddering, like the fluttering of poplar leaves on the evening breeze … he shut his eyes and prayed.

In the darkness of his mind he longed to let go, throw in the towel. What could he do against the accuracy of this counter-attack?

And then, as he felt the first upthrust of her bows beneath his body, a savage instinct gripped him. If it had to be either the destroyer or the submarine, it wasn't going to be *Rugged*. To hell with them! Now that they'd shown their intentions, he was entitled to strike back if he could regain control. They wouldn't survive another attack like the last.

"Stop blowing!"

He could distinguish his words, even above the racket in the Control Room. The bows had lifted when the air screamed into the tank. Her forefoot was swinging upwards now, up, up, away from the ravenous deeps. Mustn't break surface now … level off at a hundred feet, then fire a 'homer' from deep. That ought to teach them to laugh in church…

"Three hundred feet, sir," the First Lieutenant said breathlessly. "I've got her now, but she's coming up fast."

Peter watched the pointers on the depth gauges. The depth was decreasing; two-fifty, two-twenty … he'd better check her now. Thank heavens the planesmen were back at their stations.

"Open main vents," he ordered. "We'll have to risk the air bubbles, Number One."

Benson nodded. The guffs bursting on the surface would give away their position. But…

"Stand by numbers three and four tubes. Set to 'home'. Depth Setting, twelve feet. All-round H.E. sweep."

The expectancy in the Control Room was electric. This was their only chance. Their hunter was too accurate. It was him or *Rugged*.

"One hundred feet, sir," Benson reported.

Peter was watching Elliott, whose black head crouched low over his dials. His back stiffened suddenly. "H.E. Green one-six-o, sir. Increasing."

"In contact?" Peter asked quietly.

There was a pause while Elliott listened intently. He turned towards his captain. Then he nodded his head.

"In contact, sir. Starting her run-in again."

Peter turned towards the tube ready lamps, where the Fourth Hand, Midshipman O'Donovan, was standing, eyes mesmerised by the indicators. Number four lamp flickered. The mauve light glowed. O'Donovan wheeled round. This was new to him. Peter saw him swallow before jerking his report: "Three and four tubes ready, sir."

"Stand by!" Peter snapped, nodding at O'Donovan. "Fire by sonar bearing."

He tilted his head. Already he could hear the rumble of the destroyer working up to full speed. He watched the fruit machine: the red pointer was creeping into line with the black. So damnably slow… Would the Snotty never fire?

"*On*, sir," Elliott shouted.

A buzzer shrieked. O'Donovan stabbed the secondary firing-push. His body stiffened.

"Fire three!" he yelled down the telephone.

Phumph! the air vented back from the tube space. Peter's ears crackled. The Snotty's eyes were fixed on the hands of his stopwatch. His lips parted. There was terror in his eyes when he stared at his captain, hysteria in his voice when he spat from the tube-space phone: "Fire four!"

Phumph!

In the silence that followed they could hear the whistling of the water noises from both torpedoes. They were running, running true. It was a race now between the 'fish' and the attacking hunter. Peter stared at the compass, mesmerised. *Rugged* could never stand another hammering like the last one. He was numb. *Paralysed by fear…* He knew now what those words meant.

"Port twenty," he ordered. He *must* give his torpedoes more time. "Emergency astern!"

CHAPTER 10

Killer 'Chopper'

"Still in contact, Mikhail?"

The pilot of the helicopter took his eyes from the controls for a brief moment. He turned to watch his navigator operating the sonar winch.

"I'm lowering the dome to ten metres to see if that will improve the echoes. But we've got her all right." Mikhail looked up at Gorgi Rimov, his eyes bright above his high cheekbones. "Did you see *Narova* running in to the attack?"

Pilot First Class Gorgi Rimov shouted above the roar of the rotor. He was proud of the destroyer, proud of being part of her efficiency.

"*Da*, Mikhail. She was a grand sight. Bang on target! I saw the missiles striking the water." He looked downwards through the opening at his feet. "You better start passing ranges and bearings again. She's on the air now — ready for the next run in."

Below the swaying helicopter, the *Narova* lay stopped in the ultramarine of the Atlantic. She wallowed there, rolling still from the concentric swell caused by her mortar patterns. Her grey hull, lithe and sleek with her hard-hitting lines, seemed tiny even from this height. She was evidently waiting for her helicopter to pass fresh ranges and bearings.

"Hurry, Borovski. She's waiting." Borovski was a good navigator, but he was slow.

He had released the dome another ten metres. Now he was bending over the dials and transmitting. He looked up suddenly. Gorgi saw that he was excited. His reports were streaming into the mike of his walkie-talkie.

"Target course, two-four-eight, speed three knots. Depth thirty metres," Mikhail was shouting now. "Are you attacking?"

Gorgi gave the rotor more boost. He slowly dragged the dome nearer to the destroyer. The helicopter dipped its nose. From only fifty feet above the sea, he watched the flutter across the surface where the wind swept from his rotor.

The loudspeaker crackled above his head. "Chief calling Gorgi, Chief calling Gorgi: Stand by Run Two. Report ranges and bearings."

He flicked the switch on the walkie-talkie. He watched with amusement the heads turning towards the loudspeaker on the bridge of *Narova*. He enjoyed this game.

He'd been too long ashore, training, training, nothing but Arctic Fleet exercises in Murmansk Bay. He'd been longing for an operational appointment: even the United Nations Naval Security Force would have satisfied him — but this: this appointment was beyond his wildest hopes. They'd even detected this foreign submarine, just as the G.R.U. had predicted. That Yakov, deputy head of the organisation, was a cunning one...

"Ready to proceed," he snapped.

He shoved down the chopper's nose: she was handling beautifully. With only light airs, it was a perfect day for the hunters: a flat calm, water so clear. He eased back the throttle and lifted her a couple of feet. The fluttering of the rotors decreased in pitch and then he swung her tail around.

Da! She was perfectly placed now. Fifty metres off-track on *Narova*'s port bow; eight hundred yards ahead. Borovski could have no easier attack. Already a stream of reports was flooding from the navigator's short-range walkie-talkie.

Gorgi Rimov peered downwards at the other half of this killing machine. *Narova* was a grand sight with those clean lines, that hidden power. Nothing was out of place; the upper deck was spotless and shipshape. He watched the group of officers huddling close to the loudspeaker at the for'd end of the bridge.

He felt a surge of pride. Without him, Gorgi Rimov, there could be no accurate attack. The submarine might have slipped away already. Poor so-and-so's, he felt sorry for those men, trapped in that sardine tin. He preferred the air to that life. He leant over to peer beneath his feet. Perhaps the submarine had had enough? She might even bale out before the *coup de grâce*? Poor devils, they can't have known what hit them. Those enormous bubbles had certainly given them away.

Ah! *Narova* was lining up now; her bows were pointing directly towards them. Any moment…

"Start the attack!"

Borovski was waving his hands in delight as he repeated the order. His eyes were shining as he peered from under his flying helmet at his skipper. *There's no mistake this time*, Gorgi thought; *we've got her now. Concentrate, Gorgi. It's up to you now…*

He took the stick firmly between his hands, tested the foot pedals gingerly: a touch on the right foot pedal — ah, that was better. Her tail swung to starboard a few degrees. He could watch perfectly now.

He saw the swirl at *Narova*'s stern. The water was being thrashed white, bubbling and boiling. He saw her putting down her stern as she answered to her enormous power. Her wake snaked for a few yards, then straightened out. A green, white-laced pencil line began to streak across the ultramarine of the sea.

The bunting at her yardarms was streaming in her own wind. There was a guff of smoke at her after-funnel. (The Chief would get hell if the Old Man noticed that.) As *Narova* tore towards them, he could hear the background noises of garbled reports, orders and the hum of excited conversation.

"Six hundred metres; stand by to fire mortars!"

The captain's orders crackled in the loudspeaker above Gorgi's head. Even above the roar of the chopper's engine, you could share the electric tension from the bridge of *Narova*. If they sunk the submarine, Yakov would see to it that they were recognised: might even be a decoration for the helicopter crew…

He took a pull at himself; he *must* concentrate on the job in hand. He was doing well. He, Gorgi Rimov, mustn't let the ship down. He edged the tail round as the destroyer's bearing swept across. Only five hundred metres to go now, before passing over the target position. She'd be firing at any second now.

"*Five hundred metres*," from Borovski. There was a break in his high-pitched voice.

Gorgi could see the mortar crews at their stations, the men tensed and crouching motionless, poised to throw the firing levers at the order, "*Fire!*" With the white canvas covers thrown back, the heavy barrels of the mortars seemed black and menacing. At any second he'd catch the puff of the charges as the smoke swirled astern, see the parabolas of the projectiles as they plummeted through the air to splash beneath them. He tore away his eyes from the leaping hunter to the spot where his wire dangled down into the depths. He might even be able to see their quarry…

Then his heart leaped into his mouth. He shouted to Borovski, but no sound came. He hurled himself round, took one hand from the controls and thumped his navigator across the shoulders. He pointed downwards, jerking his hand. He remembered later the look of amazement frozen on Mikhail's face...

A few yards from where the wire sliced the sea, a line of bubbles was escaping to the surface. A distinct line ... yes, by Lenin, it was a distinct line, and it was moving. Good grief, it was streaking past their dome wire. At the same instant he heard Borovski screaming down his mike:

"Loud torpedo H.E., bearing one-six-four. *Loud torpedo H.E...*"

But Gorgi cut through the routine jargon. He screamed into the mike:

"Torpedo tracks, Chief. Right ahead, *torpedoes, torpedoes...*"

He could not take his eyes from the line of bubbles. Then he saw another track, a few yards to the left, parallel to the first. There were two, at least...

"Emergency, Chief. Emergency!" he yelled, twisting in his cockpit to watch the hideous rendezvous beneath him. "Emergency turn to port, *turn to port!* Two torpedoes approaching you..."

He could do no more. He clung to his stick, mesmerised by the duel beneath him. *Could* Narova *comb the tracks? Would she fire before the torpedoes struck? Would both adversaries destroy each other? What was he, Gorgi Rimov, to do if there was no base on which to land?* The thoughts flashed through his mind... *Narova must* swing clear — there was no future in sinking the submarine if she, the hunter, was also destroyed.

Gorgi sobbed with relief as he saw the destroyer heel suddenly to starboard. The Old Man had summed up the situation at last. He must have sighted the approaching tracks... By wrenching his wheel hard-over, he might still be able to comb the tracks...

Then Gorgi's breathing stopped. Down below him he saw the tracks of the torpedoes curving in a crescent towards the destroyer which was desperately altering course. In a tighter and tighter turn the frothing tracks curved until they merged into the confused seas of the destroyer's wake...

Gorgi suddenly realised his own danger. *Narova* was tearing towards him. In a moment she might even strike his own dome wire, she was so close. He could see the huddle of officers along the bridge rail; mesmerised by the advancing torpedo track, their heads unnaturally fixed, like spectators at a tennis match, they stared at the whispering death.

One officer was pointing with outstretched arm at the invisible dome wire which must be very close ahead now. It was Gregori, the sonar officer, the man who had been his friend on courses. Yes, Gorgi could distinguish the red hair above the pale face; he was yelling, for there was a hole where his mouth should be...

"Lift her!" he heard Mikhail screaming behind him. "Look out! Lift her, sir."

Gorgi saw his danger. He wrenched back the stick as the destroyer began sliding from view beneath him. Her bows vanished first, then the truck of her mainmast shaved his floats. Karenina! A near thing!

He could feel the thumping of his heart as he swung above the two black caverns which were her funnels. He looked down. He was immediately above her now. The torpedo tracks were one with the maelstrom of the destroyer's wake.

There was a sudden, vivid electric-blue light; an orange flash, then a wave of blistering heat. He felt the control column being torn from his grasp; felt the chopper lurch drunkenly. He remembered the wind howling past his ears, saw a fiery mass whirling up to meet him. The horizon line was spinning above his head. There was blackness, a roaring all about him as he tugged the firing lever to blow the escape door. The world flashed crimson then, and he knew no more...

CHAPTER 11

Desperate Gamble

The periscope slid upwards. Peter Sinclair's thoughts raced as he wrenched at the handles, glanced at the gauges: fifty feet and coming up fast.

Rugged was still intact. He thought their world was disintegrating when the torpedoes struck: must have been immediately above them. He glanced at the clock: eleven fifty in the forenoon. It couldn't be as late as that.

San Marco had a five-hour start then — about a hundred miles. He swore beneath his breath. They may still be alive, but Hank Jefferson was a dead duck. Then his mind began to think rationally again. If he was quick *Rugged* could catch the noon Admiralty shipping broadcast. He'd get the P.O. Tel. himself to set watch. He swung round on the stick, waiting for the lens to break surface. How uncanny the silence was: no H.E. now, no transmissions, nothing after those first terrifying moments when their world was being split asunder.

Then came the unreality of their miraculous deliverance. He wiped the sweat from his forehead and peered into the lenses as *Rugged* slid to periscope depth.

The light from the surface streamed suddenly into his eyes. He waited that split second while the smear evaporated across the glass; then, with the stick in low power, he spun round on his heel.

Ah! Something there…

He flicked the handles; the lens clicked to high power. Looked like wreckage, the pathetic remains of a stricken ship.

He'd grown used to this sight in more brutal days, but it still came as a shock. He slammed shut the handles. The helicopter might pick him up.

The periscope slid down again. He'd wait a half minute before another look. That helicopter certainly had a problem if the destroyer was sunk. Had the aircraft enough fuel to reach Fayal? Did he know his position? Well, that was his worry.

"Up periscope."

He carried out a swift aircraft sweep: nothing. He could inspect the wreckage carefully now. There could be few survivors.

"Stand by to surface, Number One. Tell the Chief I want a hull inspection when we get up top."

"Aye, aye, sir."

"There seems to be no one—"

He checked his words as the periscope swung right ahead. Something had moved amongst that wreckage, he was sure of it. Looked like a human arm. Yes, it *was* moving. Unlike the other grim flotsam that floated past the periscope, there must be a human life here... There it was again! The arm was waving frantically now, gesticulating towards the periscope. There was the head ... a black, sodden head of hair emerging from behind a bank of bobbing wooden lockers.

"As you were, Number One. There's a survivor. Poor devil..."

"Ready to surface, sir."

"Surface."

The air screamed along the high pressure lines; the bows tilted beneath Peter's feet as he began scrambling up the conning tower ladder.

"Twenty-eight feet, sir..." from somewhere below him. Number One's voice it was, calm and permanent in this nightmare world. Yet Peter's numbed mind still worked, a machine drilled by hard discipline. A mind trained to operate after the will to survive had died.

"Off one clip," he yelled at Goddard above him in the tower.

And so, ten minutes later, Peter watched the Second Coxswain haul the only survivor up the pressure hull from the oil-scummed sea. They dragged the wretch in front of him on the bridge, where he stood trembling from shock and cold. He didn't look a German: more of a Pole than a squarehead.

"Take him below," Peter said. "I'll see him later."

By the time the Chief had inspected thoroughly the pressure hull (a leak had developed around Number Five Bow-Cap, where the flange was sweated into the pressure hull) the P.O. Tel. had read his routine. His head emerged through the upper conning tower hatch. He looked pale in this sunlight; his dark eyes were smiling when he handed the signal pad to his captain.

"One unidentified, sir. The Navigating Officer's putting it on the chart now."

Peter grunted. He was worried. Apart from their existence, what was the point of survival if he'd lost track of *San Marco*? He did not dare pipe up on W/T to Admiralty or Kramer would pick up their transmissions.

"Was *San Marco* mentioned by name, or merely a whaler, P.O. Tel.?"

"No, sir," said Petty Officer James Haig, a heavily-built Londoner with black eyes. "I'm sorry, sir. They didn't mention either. Just an unidentified ship."

Peter felt the sympathy behind the man's words. His senior ratings were a grand lot: they understood the burden he had to carry.

"All right, I'll be diving in a minute. Tell the Navigator to plot a search circle, radius one hundred miles."

"Aye, aye, sir." Haig allowed himself a lingering glance around the horizon before bobbing down again into the blackness.

Then the Chief appeared over the bridge rail. He was breathless and shaking his head.

"She's a braw, wee lass, sir…"

Peter was impatient. How serious was it? Was it safe to dive again, or would he have to take her back on the surface to England? "Well, Chief?"

"There's a strain for'd, sir; nae doot aboot it."

"Is she seaworthy, man?"

"Ay, she'll do."

Peter sighed. There were moments when he could murder this dour Scot.

"Thank you, Chief. I'll dive now."

Ewan Craig nodded, then lowered himself slowly through the hatch.

"Ye'll no gae too deep, sir?" he observed, as his head slipped into the blackness. "An awfu' peety to strain the guid Lorrrd's patience ower muckle."

Peter strode to the bridge side. He stabbed at the diving alarm. "Clear the bridge," he yelled. "Dive, dive, dive!"

It had been a difficult guess. But now Elliott had picked up faint H.E. right ahead. Peter stooped over his H.S.D.'s shoulders and picked up the dual headphones. Every half hour he'd stopped *Rugged* to listen.

"On *now*, sir."

Peter held his breath, waiting for silence. This was the moment they had been chasing at thirty-five knots for the past seven hours. Each Admiralty shipping bulletin had confirmed their estimate: this unidentified ship was steering north, due north.

The last bulletin had not mentioned her. Peter was now on his own. If this shadow they had been overhauling was some innocuous steamer, he might as well return to base to face the music. Then he would have more disasters to face: the ramming and his accusations against the Germans, their NATO allies; his inability to carry out even the simplest of tasks — the shadowing of a merchant ship. His disappearance without reporting his position…

Joe Croxton would be powerless to save him at a court martial, high ranking though he was. Peter's mission was Top Secret (Joe had warned him of that at the outset). No, the run of the play was against him. He'd forced his hand too hard. There were better C.O.s than him, he had to face it. And they were jostling for position in the promotion stakes.

Then very gradually into his fevered mind came the persistent throb of strange propellers.

"I've got her!" he shouted.

Elliott looked up sharply at his captain. Peter pulled himself together as he watched the H.S.D. counting, against a stopwatch, the beats of the stranger's propellers. Elliott's head was nodding; his thumb jerked suddenly and then he looked at the motionless hands of the watch. He turned slowly towards his captain.

"Diesel, sir," he said. His black eyes were bright. "One-two-eight revolutions, sir."

"What were the revs of the ship we followed down Channel?" Peter held his breath while he waited for the answer to his question.

"One-two-eight, sir."

Peter wrenched off the headset. "Half ahead," he snapped. "Steer three-six-o."

Elliott's estimate of distance was six miles: about six minutes at *Rugged's* dived full speed. He'd better reduce, in case the stranger *was San Marco* and *was* listening.

He pushed the hope from him. It would be too cruel to be disappointed now. Surely the stranger must be *San Marco*? But why this course?

She was steering up the twenty-ninth longitudinal; by dawn tomorrow she'd be eight hundred miles due west of southern Ireland. Why the dickens did she steam down to Fayal first? If she *was San Marco*, she must have some compelling reason to steam down to the Azores before altering to her real course to the northward. Perhaps she was making for Iceland? He swore beneath his breath, pushing away the absurd idea. He'd got nothing out of the helicopter pilot, apart from the strange fact that the man was a Russian. But why Russians here?

The hands of the clock crawled around the dial. Nineteen twenty-five: the last minutes of twilight. The H.E. was loud now, right ahead. He'd stop *Rugged* and slide up to have a look while there was still enough light.

"Stop motor. Periscope depth."

His heart was hammering against his ribs when the glass finally splashed through the surface. It was very dark already. At first, he could not distinguish sea from horizon. Then suddenly he saw her, a dark shape looming right ahead. His heart leapt into his mouth. He slammed shut the handles.

"One hundred feet," he snapped. "It's her all right, Number One." The nervous smile vanished from his face. "She's showing no lights. She's darkened."

Ian Taggart, Sub-Lieutenant, R.N.R., Navigating Officer of H.M. Nuclear Submarine *Rugged*, sprawled over his chart table. His back was to the Control Room and his shoulders were hunched as he crouched over the illuminated plot. His lips were pursed. No one could see him from here. He'd done all he could by insinuation but still the Old Man obstinately stuck to his theory.

There were moments now when he, Ian Taggart, was forced to admit that Sinclair was losing his grip. In these moments, the Navigating Officer of *Rugged* felt horribly disloyal. He had tried to shove the thoughts from his mind. He had succeeded to date. But now his loyalty was being strained to the uttermost.

Sinclair was on a fool's errand. It was rough on Jefferson if he had been abducted by some clandestine movement: hell's teeth, Germany was full of spies. The nation revelled in that game.

But why drag this priceless weapon, this nuclear submarine up into these latitudes on what was no more than an absurd hunch? Why, the last sight he'd taken through the periscope was two days ago, on the eleventh (and he'd only snatched a sun-run-mer. alt. then). Visibility was always low now. And it was growing cold.

Their present D.R. was too absurd to believe. They'd altered course an hour ago to follow the H.E. ahead. This took them straight up the Denmark Strait — how absurd could you get? Tomorrow at this time they'd be between Jan Mayen island and Scoresby Sund, if they maintained this course. And then where to, for Pete's sake? If she turned east, *San Marco* (for certainly it was she) would almost have completed three sides of a rectangle...

Ian Taggart shook his head. He turned round to watch his captain, the man in whom he had once so much trust. But Peter Sinclair had left the Control Room for his cabin. Number One was taking the helicopter pilot to the captain for another interrogation.

The prisoner seemed decent enough, though surly. He'd given his name as Gorgi Rimov. He was lucky to have been picked up, for he was the only living survivor when *Rugged* surfaced. The navigator had been drowned when the chopper had hit the water. Rimov had been flung clear.

The survivor was an odd bird. He gave away nothing. His conversation consisted of the word: '*niet*'. The troops called him Nit. Hawkins, the oldest Able Seaman in the boat, had taken the prisoner under his wing. They were 'jollying' the poor wretch, and already there were signs of a softening in his attitude. Hawkins would get something out of him before the days were much older. But (and Ian Taggart scratched his head) why had they been savaged by *Russians* who were, after all, partners in this United Nations Naval Security Force? And was it a coincidence that this hunting force was ready and waiting for *Rugged* when she sneaked into the area? Did this Communist force know of *San Marco* which was, from what the captain said, a German ship? Perhaps she was an East German?

Taggart turned to his chart again. He picked up his dividers and drove them savagely into the chart. Wretched Sinclair! The poor fellow was going to take such a tumble shortly. He'd be the laughing stock of The Trade, and this would reflect on *Rugged*. The captain could not afford to lose face in these days of cut-throat promotion. There'd been rumours already.

CHAPTER 12

Desolate Landfall

"Captain, sir."

Peter was scrambling from his bunk even before he felt the pressure of Hawkins's fist on his shoulder. He glanced at the clock over the door lintel: 1156. What day was it? Ah, yes, the fifteenth of June — nearly the longest day of the year. As he stumbled down into the Control Room, he gathered his thoughts. They were somewhere off the Greenland coast and still steering north. He saw the bewilderment on Benson's face.

"I've reduced to 'slow', sir. Sonar reports *San Marco*'s revs are decreasing."

Peter nodded. He strode to the chart. Taggart's E.P. at 0400 was pencilled neatly across their track. About eighty degrees north. He'd never been so far north. Well inside the Arctic Circle. Thank heavens it was midsummer. At least there was daylight throughout the twenty-four hours. Navigation was difficult and Taggart was to be congratulated on including a chart folio of this area.

Rugged had sighted land only once: on the thirteenth of June off Kap Brewster. The coast had been a shadow in the swirling mists. Now, at noon on the fifteenth, their quarry was slowing down at last.

"Target altering course to port, sir."

"Speed?"

"Eight-o revs, sir. About six knots."

"Follow her. Stop motor. Periscope depth."

They could feel the motion of the swell even at eighty feet. *Rugged* was a plaything in the grip of these restless seas. She was rolling heavily as she planed up across the swell.

"Forty feet, sir."

Peter flicked his thumb. He squinted through the eyepieces.

"Thirty-three feet, sir."

Ah, that was better. Number One could afford to be a trifle shallow in these seas.

"Bearing THAT, *San Marco*." He swivelled round on his heel, "and THAT, a sheer cliff with an icecap. Looks like a Cape."

He could see clearly now: *San Marco* had no bow wave, though she was still under way. She, too, was rolling in this mountainous cross-swell. *Rugged* was on her port quarter now, about three miles off. At least they were safe from detection in these conditions…

"Permission to flood 'Q', sir?"

Peter slammed the handles of the periscope. He glanced at the gauges. Thirty feet. Good grief, they were breaking surface! Once the fin broke surface, there'd be no stopping her. She was a cow to get down again: she'd wallow in the troughs, visible for miles.

"Flood 'Q'. Full ahead," Peter yelled. "For Pete's sake keep her tail down, Number One. If her stern cocks up, we've had it."

Peter took over. He glared at the gauges to smother his anger. Thirty feet — she was just holding. A breaking sea now and she'd be hurled upwards like a toy… Hank's death sentence.

Number One had been careless. They'd navigated for thousands of miles with the utmost care — and now this…

"Twenty-nine feet, sir."

He could hear the seas crashing against the sides of the fin, feel the pounding on the pressure hull. There was a crash from the fore-ends of gear breaking loose.

"'Q' flooding, sir," Saunders, the E.R.A., reported. "Permission to vent inboard?"

"No. Vent outboard. Won't show in this weather. No aircraft about."

"Twenty-eight feet, sir." He could feel the anxiety in Number One's reports. This was a desperate moment. Breaking surface was a crime hated by submariners, though sometimes it could not be prevented.

Peter felt the hull trembling beneath his feet as she gathered speed.

"Twenty-seven feet, sir."

Peter dared not look at the gauges. The upper edge of the fin must be showing now… Well, he had tried, at least… Luck was running against him. You couldn't do more than your best, could you?

"She's going, sir."

Peter glanced at Saunders. His eyes were bright, his pale skin glistened over his cheekbones.

Rugged was taking on a steep bow-down angle now, just as he'd feared. Her stern must be showing — dammit, Number One, for Pete's sake!

"More dive on the after-planes," Peter yelled. "You *must* keep her tail down."

The banging of the loose gear could be heard above her wild rolling. Peter grasped the ladder. This was appalling, inefficient submarining. Blind rage swept through him.

"Flood everything you've got, Number One. *You've got to get her down.*"

But diving a boat, once she has broken surface in wild seas, is no easy matter. With her screw racing, it may take minutes.

Her propeller was racing, cavitating in the troughs. It would suddenly jerk from the water to thresh wildly in the air. Even the governor could not stop this fiendish torque. The boat shuddered and groaned at each wild spasm.

She would not go down: air must be trapped underneath the casing.

"Open main vents," Peter shouted. "Full ahead."

Above the crashing of the seas came the rumble of full power. Even if the propeller flew apart in mid air, he *must* get her down. God, this was awful. She must be plainly visible by now. He could not stand because of the angle.

"Twenty-eight feet, sir ... twenty-nine..."

Peter forced his eyes to the gauges.

"All main vents checked open, sir."

The calmness of Saunders's voice was comforting. A sound man, this Cornishman.

"Thirty feet, sir."

He must be careful now, or she'd go with a rush. Couldn't afford to make more noise than necessary, certainly not blow Main Ballast. He snapped his fingers. The stick slid upwards.

"Thirty-four feet, sir ... thirty-five..."

"Up periscope."

A white circle of light burst upon Peter's eyes. Her bows were underwater anyway, and maybe so was her stern now... Perhaps there was a chance...

He swung on to *San Marco*'s bearing. His face cracked into a smile.

"You're lucky, Number One," he drawled drawing back from the eye pieces. "Come and have a look."

Benson grabbed the handles and peered for a moment.

"Thank God," he whispered, as he slammed shut the handles. "That rain squall came at the right time."

Peter was smiling. "Blow 'Q'," he ordered. "A bit of luck at last. We can do with it."

It was not until 0530 on the sixteenth that *San Marco* stopped. She had altered course to the south-west shortly after midnight. Now that she was proceeding at slow speed, *Rugged* had closed up on her. Tonight was as bright as day. Peter could see now for miles. Visibility had cleared to that peculiar transparency and clarity of the Arctic where the atmosphere is cold and rare.

To starboard, white clouds were encircling the distant mountains; beneath that mantle of billowing whiteness there spread a range of hills with, strangely, an olive-green drabness about them. This hinterland stretched into the distance as far as the eye could see.

They were nudging their way up a broad inlet. To port, the mountains seemed much nearer, much steeper. Yet, at their feet there spread this same green carpet. Perhaps it was tundra or some type of moss? What was Greenland's vegetation in these latitudes? Surely nothing grew in this desolation? There was an ice line half a mile from shore; a menacing inhospitable coast.

At midnight, *San Marco* rounded Danmark Fjord, a grey finger disappearing into the white mists. *Rugged* continued shadowing at less than two miles. Peter dared not lose her now. There was a ripple on the water so he could freely use his periscope.

At 0400 Peter was wondering how much farther his quarry would proceed up the fjord. She'd already entered some fifteen miles and now, dead ahead, their passage seemed to be blocked by a wall of pack ice, thirty feet high.

The fjord had narrowed. The cliffs to port were only half a mile away; to starboard, the northern side of the fjord was less than two miles distant.

San Marco had nudged cautiously towards this pack ice. *Rugged* had been pushing through loose ice for the past three days. It had been on the thirteenth that Brocklebank, Officer of the Watch at periscope depth, had sighted the first iceberg in the Denmark Strait: they had grown in size, the farther north that *Rugged* sailed.

It was this ice line which had determined *San Marco*'s course. Peter could understand it now: why she suddenly veered to the north-east north of Jan Mayen island, then cut back towards Wendels Sea. At this time of the year the ice was at its minimum, the pack having drifted south into the northern Atlantic. This must be the reason, Peter thought as he turned over the problem in his mind for the thousandth time, this must be the answer to two unanswered questions.

Why was *San Marco* so broad in the beam and of such massive strength? In Hamburg he'd put it down to her whaling occupation. But the whale had gone south. So why did this strange ship, with her dry-dock bows, come to these distant shores, these wicked, inhospitable fastnesses in June?

If it was seal she was after (he'd seen schools of them during the past few days), why such a ponderous and gigantic ship? And why, for heaven's sake, should Kramer, who hated the sea, sail to this notoriously dangerous coast?

These icebergs would have deterred better men than Kramer. Peter had given them a wide berth. Their blue-green precipices, plunging deeply into the black water beneath them, were large enough to swallow a modern skyscraper. Through *Rugged*'s periscope, the swell breaking lazily upon the glistening ice was impressive enough. To Kramer, their silence and immensity must have been terrifying as his ship ploughed northward through the mists, though the low-lying fog blanketing the sea like a shroud. As Peter watched, *San Marco*'s screws suddenly thrashing as she went astern, these facts were no answer to his confusion of mind.

The rattle of *San Marco*'s anchor cable dinned against *Rugged*'s pressure hull. Peter took this opportunity to take a sounding: twenty-six fathoms. Deep water for anchoring. *Rugged* had better lie off to the northward to await developments. He took her round in a broad sweep to gain bearing on *San Marco*'s starboard quarter. At three miles, he rounded up.

"Up periscope."

In high-power he could see her plainly. Her cable party was still securing the fo'c'sle. He could see them flinging their arms around their chests to keep their circulation going.

It was very calm up top — like a mirror, grey and forbidding, with silvery streaks running towards the ice line two miles away. The sky was a steely blue. The eastern horizon was now concealed by the point round which they'd come. They were, in fact, entirely screened from seaward by the northern finger of ice circling away to the north-east.

Ahead lay the ice wall, wreathed in mist. In these proportions *San Marco* seemed a toy boat floating on the surface of a tub as she came to her anchor beneath the overhanging mountains. Black slabs of granite were these giants, whitecapped on their crests, their flanks plunging vertically into the ice fringe at their bases.

There was so little wind. A ribbon of smoke rose vertically from one of *San Marco*'s funnels. She must be shutting down,

Peter guessed, as only her generator discharges were cascading over the side now. She must be preparing to stop here.

Then, while considering whether to close any nearer, he stepped back from the periscope. He slowly closed the handles. He stared at the second hand crawling round the face of the brass clock above the helmsman. Silently he stood there, his heart racing. He could not believe his eyes. He snapped his fingers. There was a *hiss!* and the steel tube slid upwards again.

"Well!"

He gripped the handles to hide his emotion.

"Have a look, Number One," he said. "D'you see anything?"

The hands were tired, bored by these days of shadowing. They wished the Old Man would get a hustle on so that they could go to breakfast. But Elliott was clasping his headset to his ears, as his fingers twirled the ebonite knob above the glowing dial. Benson stepped back from the periscope.

"Yes, sir," he said, his face drained of colour. "But—"

"What do you see?" Peter snapped.

"A submarine, sir, surfacing just ahead of *San Marco*."

Elliott's voice crackled from the sonar compartment. "Submarine blowing tanks, sir. Red one-o."

Peter nodded. "That's what I thought I saw, Number One." He was grinning. So his eyes weren't playing tricks after these long days of strain and radar shutdown.

Peter glanced around the Control Room. The crew were tensed now, incredulity etched upon their faces. Even Taggart's mouth hung open. A look of relief, almost of happiness, was on his face. His lips were moving.

Peter's mouth twitched. It had been a strain, but now he was vindicated. All along, even from Number One down to Able Seaman Hawkins, he felt he'd been losing their confidence. Peter moved across to the chart. He met Taggart's eyes.

121

"What were you saying, Pilot?"

"Thank God, sir," the young Scot whispered. "Thank God."

Peter smiled. Sentimental, some of these people. Too soft. You couldn't mix submarining with emotion.

"Submarine blowing tanks, sir."

Peter Sinclair was half asleep in his cabin. He'd been snatching at sleep while the Officer of the Watch took *Rugged* up and down a line two miles off *San Marco*. Even in his semi-consciousness the reports from the Control Room registered in his mind, through the speaker above his bunk. He reached the Control Room as the Third Hand shouted for him.

"Captain in the Control Room!"

Peter snatched the periscope from Spink's hands. "Put me on, Sub."

Instinctively he swept round full circle. Years of training, years of safety drill … aircraft were unlikely up here. Then suddenly he stiffened. He flicked into high power.

"Blow me down, Sub," he said softly. "Not only another U-boat but an aircraft as well."

The periscope streaked down into the well as he turned to Sub-Lieutenant Spink, his gangling, good-natured Third Hand.

"She's got skids on, Sub."

Spink looked worried. "Good grief, sir! Where's she got 'em? On her conning tower?"

Peter looked away. The chap really was thick…

"The aircraft, you ass! It's got skids instead of wheels."

Spink grunted and scratched the side of his head.

"*San Marco* was quick in landing her, sir. Couldn't see a helicopter through the periscope."

"No catapult," said Peter quietly. He held his chin and looked quizzically about him.

"Send for Nit… Get Rimov here," he ordered. "He might understand my Russian."

Two minutes later the Russian prisoner stood between the periscopes, Hawkins and the Second Coxswain on either side of him.

Peter spoke haltingly in his best Russian. (He was secretly proud of his linguistic powers; he'd passed out well in the Interpreter's Course.)

"Look, Rimov," he said sharply, handing him the periscope. "What sort of aircraft is that? Russian or German?"

The prisoner hesitated. Then, at a nudge from Hawkins, he gingerly took hold of the extended arms of the periscope. Peter watched closely the intelligent face, saw the nerve twitching at the side of his sensitive forehead.

"Well?"

"German," Rimov whispered as he stepped back. The periscope slid downwards. "Storck Seventeen."

"Certain?" Peter snapped.

"*Da*, sir." The Russian grinned. "There's one thing on which we Russians agree with you Englishmen, sir!"

"Yes?"

It was difficult not to be disarmed by the Russian's charm.

"We don't trust Germans."

Peter smiled. He couldn't deny it.

"But why did *you* have a crack at *us*?" Peter asked his prisoner for the hundredth time. Then, even as he blurted the question, the answer came into his mind. Of course: these German U-boats. Rimov was grinning.

"We knew of these German submarines, sir. We did not know their business."

"I see," Peter said. "Take him away, Weston."

He turned to look again. Incredible. Perhaps they'd learn more if they waited.

The second U-boat lay stopped, a hundred yards from *San Marco*'s bow; overhead, twisting, diving and playing high jinks, the little plane zoomed. This rendezvous had evidently been expected. Then, as Peter watched, plumes of spray spouted from *San Marco*'s bows.

"Just like main vents," he murmured. "Her bows are settling in the water, dammit."

During the next twenty minutes, Peter witnessed a strange sight. U-boat Number Two (there was a large white numeral painted on her conning tower) emerged at full buoyancy from *San Marco*.

"She's just a floating dock," Peter exclaimed. "Look, Number One. The U-boats are exchanging places. Number Five's going in now."

Peter grinned. Amazement was spreading across his First Lieutenant's face.

"This explains a lot, sir," Benson said. "The secrecy, the course…"

"Uh-huh. I reckon *San Marco*'s a depot ship to store and maintain those U-boats," Peter said.

"I wonder how many more submarines there are up here."

"We'll soon see." Peter Sinclair was grinning. He was his old self again.

"That's what we're going to find out, Number One." He turned to his Navigating Officer. "Pilot, get the course of the U-boat steering towards the ice barrier. I'm one hundred and twenty degrees on her starboard bow. Look, dammit! she's swung under it!"

Benson exchanged places at the periscope. He gave a low whistle, then turned to his captain. "You going to follow, sir?"

Peter was enjoying himself. "That's just what we're going to do. And I'll lay you a bet Kramer's in that U-boat."

"Probably got Hank with him, sir. But where the devil are they going? What can there be ashore in this godforsaken spot?"

Peter was scratching his head. "It's only ice, when all's said and done. Why, for Pete's sake, does Kramer come all this way to land on a frozen, uncharted fjord? And why kidnap Hank? Why bring him here?"

Benson spread his hands. "Kramer's got to come back to the *San Marco*, hasn't he, sir? If I remember rightly, he doesn't enjoy the life of a submariner."

Peter was silent. You could hear the ticking of the bulkhead clock. He turned to his First Lieutenant.

"You've given me an idea, Number One. By God, you've given me an idea." He was grinning and his eyes were shining. "When's evening twilight, Pilot?"

Taggart glanced at his navigational notebook. "Eleven twenty tonight, sir."

Peter nodded. "Lay off a course out of the fjord, Pilot. Take me out of this madhouse." He turned to his First Lieutenant. "Send the painter to me, Number One."

"The *painter*, sir?"

"Yes, damn you, the painter." Peter was grinning. "And Number One…"

"Sir?"

"Exercise Boarding Party. I'll be needing as many armed pirates as I can."

Benson was shaking his head slowly from side to side.

"When, sir?"

"Twilight tonight. You better get cracking."

CHAPTER 13

Drake's Men

Peter's insides felt like water. As he looked around him in the red lighting, he knew the meaning of fear. In less than five minutes he would be either dead or alive; and so would his crew. No half-measures about this next half hour: it was *San Marco* or *Rugged*, with the possibility (and only a possibility) of Hank's life as the prize. In the subdued glow of the red lighting, the sudden transformation of the Control Room was eerie.

The red glow bathed the blackened faces of the boarding party and transformed his sailors into murderous pirates. The whites of George Stack's eyes, the tough ex-gunlayer, gleamed as he rolled them in the gloom. He was standing in silence at the bottom of the ladder, an F.N. crooked into his arm. Around his belt hung a row of stick-grenades, at his hip the blue steel of a Commando knife. A tin hat was on his head; he was checking the safety catch of the F.N., the Belgian automatic rifle, when he turned towards the party.

"All ready?" he croaked.

There were murmurs from the band of cut-throats in the fore-ends where they were making last minute adjustments to their weapons. In the cramped confinement between the racks, torpedoes in all of them except Number Six which held a folboat, there was much confusion.

"Ready, sir," Stack reported to the boarding officer, Midshipman Michael O'Donovan, the Fourth Hand. The Snotty looked at his Captain.

"Follow me up," Peter snapped. "Open the lower lid, Signalman in the tower."

Peter patted the Colt at his hip. Then he turned to his First Lieutenant: "As soon as we're up, Number One, come to full buoyancy without further orders, but flood 'Q': we may need it in a hurry. Any questions?"

The First Lieutenant's face was set. He shook his head.

"Stand by to surface."

Peter followed Goddard up the ladder and into the conning tower. He climbed upwards, hand over hand in the darkness until he heard Goddard's breathing above him. He felt the man's shoes scraping against his head.

"Ready, Signalman?"

Peter felt his heart hammering against his ribs. They were within two cables of the whaling ship. In the twilight they might get away with it.

"Ready, sir…"

"What signal are you going to flash?"

"Operating procedure, sir."

"Right. Off one clip."

The long-handled clip rattled as the jaws fell free.

"Surface!"

Peter felt Stack's hands on the rungs beneath him, heard the muttered curses. Then suddenly *Rugged* was on her way upwards, swooping to the surface.

"Twenty-five feet, sir…" from somewhere far below. "Twenty — eighteen…"

A whistle blew, Goddard wrenched off the last clip; water splashed in Peter's face as the cold of the night pierced him; and then he was scrambling up the rungs, clambering through the hatch to fumble frantically for the voicepipe cock at the fore-end of the bridge. As the water gurgled through the free-flood holes under his feet he heard the patter of men stealing to their hidden stations in the fin. He peered over the bridge rail.

Directly ahead, on the end of *Rugged*'s stern, towered the bows of *San Marco*. Her gigantic structure must have been twenty feet above the fin; a catwalk joined the two spurs on either bow. *Rugged*'s conning tower might just clear.

"Make the signal!"

He heard his whisper above the beating of his heart. Goddard started flashing with his blue lamp over the edge of the bridge rail, its pale light bathing the white pendant number on the port side of the fin: a large numeral '3'.

Peter leaned over the voicepipe.

"Officer of the Watch and mooring party on the bridge," he said softly.

The silence of the darkened submarine was uncanny. The blowers were running now, bringing her rapidly to full buoyancy.

Wish to goodness San Marco *would answer. We're too close.*

"Keep flashing, Goddard."

"Aye, aye, sir. Shall I try the white light?"

Peter hesitated. Would it be too presumptuous? Then he realised his mistake. These Germans believed themselves undiscovered, in a secret corner of an uncharted fjord.

"Yes, do that."

The lantern clicked. A white light lit up the loom of the ship.

Brocklebank was whispering in the darkness. "Mooring party closed up, sir."

Peter grunted. This was a situation he hadn't bargained for. *San Marco* had not even set lookouts. Then from out of the darkness a German voice hailed: "*Achtung!* Who are you? What do you want?"

Peter cleared his throat; cupped his hands, yelled in German:

"Number Three. Why aren't you ready for me? I'm coming in now."

The man in the darkness was grumbling to himself. "The captain never told me you were expected. Hold on; I'll get things moving." He paused. "D'you need Both Watches?"

"*Nein.* I can see. Won't need the lights either. Don't want to cause trouble."

The guttural laughter boomed round them from the dock.

"*Danke schön, mein Kommandant,*" floated from *San Marco.*

Peter yelled back: "Hurry. We've waited long enough."

"*Ja ... ja.*"

The words were carried away on the wind. Footsteps rang upon the iron decks.

"Stand by, mooring party," Peter whispered to Brocklebank, whose bulk was silhouetted against the skyline. "You look hideous."

In his nervousness, it was all Peter could do to stop laughing. Brocklebank, with the whites of his eyes rolling in his boot-blacked face, looked the most wicked scoundrel upon whom Peter had ever clapped eyes.

The lip-lap of the sea against the pressure hull was the only sound; nothing now except the deep breathing of his hidden pirates. *I must remember to give my orders in German*, Peter thought. He turned to Brocklebank.

"Talk only in German, if you can," he whispered. "Tell the Signalman to keep his mouth shut."

This waiting was the worst part. Perhaps the Huns were checking up on them? Were they walking into a trap?

Then suddenly there was a familiar roar: escaping air, the gerfuffle of main vents blowing. A light glowed on the gantry above. At any rate, they were flooding up. He could see no sentries, no weapons trained upon them.

The bows of *San Marco* were beginning to settle. He could see the water climbing up the sloping floor of the dock even as her bows sank. The swell was negligible here. Only a thin white line of surf etched the sides of the dock. Ahead of *Rugged* stretched a vast swimming bath.

"They're calling up from the bridge, sir," Goddard whispered.

"Give him an 'R'."

"Aye, aye, sir."

The shutter of the lamp clattered. The ray of light pierced the gloom.

"Mooring party on the casing, Brock."

"Aye, aye, sir."

The gangling body uncurled itself, climbed over the bridge rail. Four figures slipped after him, heaving lines in their hands. They were dressed in sea-going rig: capless and in overalls, no badges on their arms.

"Slow ahead, Cox'n," Peter murmured softly to the figure in the darkness below him. "Take her in."

As *Rugged*'s bow inched forwards between the two sponsons towering above them, Peter saw a man directly above him. He was yawning and pulling a scarf about his head. Ahead was the bridge which formed the end of the dock. On either side were two cranes, gangways dangling from their jibs.

"Nothing to port," Peter whispered to the Coxswain. "Steady."

The gantry was sliding along the fore-casing now. A heavy line plummeted down to the casing where Hawkins grabbed it. He waved his hand and walked nonchalantly for'd. He began hauling in the line, hand over hand, until he had enough to take a turn round the for'd bollards. Two arc lights snapped on below the jib of each crane. Their lights swung crazily, casting weird shadows across the dock.

Peter saw the gantry sliding towards the bridge. A shadow shielded him from sight and then the fin cleared — by less than three feet. He kept his head averted as he slid beneath the man on the gantry. He held his breath. He turned cautiously as they drew clear. He could see his two men at the stern, one hauling in the stern line. Thirty yards to go... He spoke softly down the voicepipe.

"Stop motor."

The tension was electric. The steel plates of the dock were sliding by less rapidly now. A white lifebuoy on the dockside slowly drew alongside.

"Slow astern."

He peered aft, waiting for the Coxswain at her stern. He heard the rumble, felt the sudden trembling of the hull. He glanced at the dockside. The lifebuoy was sliding to a halt; it was stationary.

"Stop motor."

He whispered hoarsely down the voicepipe: a German was level with him on the dockside. He was silhouetted plainly against the indigo-blue of this half-night.

"*Das ist gut.*"

The man's voice was high-pitched. Was Peter imagining it, or was the man suspicious? The submarine captain had better say something. He half-turned towards the man, but shouted towards the fore-casing party.

"*Danke schön.*" He grabbed his megaphone. He shouted unintelligibly, in guttural German, towards the bows. Able Seaman Hawkins was backing up the fore-spring. O'Riley unused to being in a berthing party, was getting out the headrope. There was the whine of electric motors, and the shadows started dancing crazily. The crane was clanking towards the bridge. Simultaneously, the jib was being lowered until it plumbed the fore-casing, a few yards ahead of the fin. Below it stood Hawkins, beckoning to O'Riley. Peter held his breath: one word of English now…

"Welcome aboard *San Marco, Herr Kapitan.*"

The German words boomed at him from the far end of the dock. A big man was rolling towards the conning tower. By his authoritative voice, he was probably the captain.

"*Danke schön, Herr Kapitan,*" Peter yelled upwards. He spun on his heel and whispered into the darkness of the fin: "Get your men on to the fore-casing. The Signalman's covering you." He hissed at Goddard. "Stand by, Signalman. Open fire at the least sign of resistance."

He saw the man pick up his F.N.; watched him slip off the safety catch; caught the gleam of the barrel resting along the bridge rail.

"Now!" Peter whispered hoarsely. "The brow's across."

It seemed a lifetime before O'Donovan reached the head of the brow. Hawkins was leaning down, securing its inboard end. Any second now… Peter drew his revolver.

"I'll take the man on the gantry," he growled at Goddard. "Leave the gangway to the boarding officer. Shift target to that group coming down the other side."

So they had turned out the Watch, had they? His heart hammered against his ribs as he swallowed. So far things had been too good to be true. How many in the ship's company? He watched Goddard's bunch traversing to the starboard side. He could cut down the whole bunch if he wanted … they weren't even armed.

He spun round as he heard a pattering along the wet steel plating. The boarding party were swarming up the steel ladders now, stealth and concealment jettisoned. Suddenly, unable to smother the tension another second, he heard Jack Weston's deep voice echoing across the dock.

"The Navy's here. Come on, boys!"

There was an answering roar and Peter's heart swelled. It was *Cossack* and *Altmark* over again. A confused shouting broke out along the dockside to starboard. He saw the men stop, hesitate, begin to retrace their tracks.

The Signalman's body stiffened. An ear-splitting stutter jerked by Peter's ear. A blue fire jumped; green tracers arced towards the cluster of men. A scream rent the twilight: then slowly the group melted where it stood. A man shouted, threw up his hands, then collapsed over the guard rail where he remained, hanging above the dock.

Peter spun round: the man who had been on the gantry crouched as he ran along the dockside towards the fin. Peter waited until he was abreast of him. He slowly raised his Colt .45, waited until the front edge of the dark shape crossed his sight. He squeezed the trigger.

The kick jerked his elbow. He fired again, the flash blinding him. The man crumpled, slid slowly to the plating, then slithered over the dockside. There was a splash alongside.

Peter was anxious. The more shindy there was, the more chance of rousing suspicions ashore. He jumped to the for'd edge of the bridge. He tilted the rim of his tin hat, held the Colt in his right hand. His nerves were tingling: he was in no mood to be an Aunt Sally for some marksman through one of those bridge scuttles. It was comforting to feel Goddard closing up on the other side of him. He leant his F.N. across the lip of the bridge. Smoke was still curling from its barrel.

"Too easy, sir," Goddard growled. "Almost as if they was expecting us, like."

Peter remained silent. The same thought was crossing his mind. He wished O'Donovan and Jack Weston would get a hustle on. Thank God each man knew his own job. The P.O. Tel. might have reached the wireless room by now. They might yet capture the ship. Only surprise could succeed.

Then a shout hailed him across the shadows: "Fourth Hand here, sir," a cheery voice yelled. "I've got the captain. He's making a nuisance of himself. May I shoot him?"

Peter grinned in the shadows. Bloodthirsty rascal...

"No, keep him. How's things going? Buck up, haven't much time."

For answer there was a growl from the other side: "*Rugged* ahoy! Second Cox'n speaking, sir." Peter could not see Jack Weston.

"*Rugged* here," Peter yelled back.

"We've locked 'em all in their messdeck, sir. I've battened the bulkhead doors; left Smith and O'Connor on guard. What orders now, please sir?"

He made it sound a routine job, a parade ground manoeuvre. Weston could never have enough excitement.

"How many?" Peter yelled back.

"Eighteen for'd, sir. Seven in the Engine Room."

Peter hesitated. Was that really the total?

"Is that the lot?"

"So far, sir."

"Continue to search the ship with the boarding officer. When completed, return here to make your reports. Hurry, we haven't much time."

"Aye, aye, sir."

Peter stamped his feet. No, there wasn't enough time. Kramer might return in the U-boat at any moment, and there was much to do before then. So far success was complete. But until the P.O. Tel. got back, until *Rugged*'s own W/T office made its report, it was impossible to know whether *San Marco* had alerted the shore base. He leant over the voicepipe: " Control Room?"

" Control Room, sir."

"Ask the W/T monitor whether there has been any enemy transmission on local waves."

If, even now, there was but one transmission, the game would be up. It was as simple as that. Instinctively he looked over his shoulder, along the after-casing towards the open sea. The ice pack was gleaming white in the twilight. It seemed close. He'd better get cracking.

"Stand by to slip," he shouted down the voicepipe. "First Lieutenant on the bridge."

CHAPTER 14

Death Sentence

"Bring in the prisoner."

The domed head did not look up from the desk. Under the central light, the pink smoothness of the bald pate glistened. Von Kramer felt content. Things were going even better than he had dared hope. He watched his aide scurrying from the room: he enjoyed keeping the youngsters hopping.

He pushed back his chair, stood up and braced his back. He raised his arms, flexed the muscles and felt a quick resurgence of energy. He might be nearly fifty, but he was certainly tough. He felt the muscles rippling beneath the tunic as he moved to the insulated window. He was looking forward to this interrogation: this American was a tough nut to crack. All the more enjoyable, therefore — a challenge to Kramer's skill. He had several new techniques he had not yet tried out: they had made great advances in mental processing since Belsen.

So far the American had held out. The man was an idiot; he knew something all right; yet he refused to talk. He, von Kramer, seldom failed in these duties (he smiled to himself when he remembered that elderly scientist — the little man had held out just long enough to make it pleasurable), but there was little hope of this with Jefferson. He'd die too quickly. But he'd squeal. Himmel, he'd make the swine squeal.

There was a knock on his door. He remained staring through the window. From here he could enjoy the grandeur of the scenery; he could emphasise the futility of resistance from here. There was no escape across that desolation.

"Come in," he shouted. "What're you waiting for?"

He heard a shuffling behind him, the suppressed cursing of the guard who had lugged the prisoner along. He turned slowly on his heel to relish the sight.

The American could barely stand. Though over one metre ninety, the fellow seemed to have shrunk. (*Hermann must have been overdoing it a bit. I must remember to promote him. I'll send for him before returning to Europe.*)

The man's face, too, had altered. Amazing what pain and lack of food could do, combined with persuasion. He sauntered towards the American and stood close to him, his hands behind his back and rocking on the soles of his feet. He turned towards Hermann; raised his eyebrows quizzically.

The young officer clicked his heels. His jack-boots were shining, Kramer noted, his black hair was faultlessly parted, his swastika clean, his black shirt freshly laundered. A credit to his unit. Hermann was shaking his close-cropped head.

"*Nein, Herr Kommandant.*"

Kramer could not suppress the feeling of excitement. He allowed a smile of anticipation to wreathe across his face.

"Leave him to me, *Herr Leutnant*," he said softly. "I will try once more before I leave. If I fail," he shrugged his massive shoulders. "If I should fail, you know what to do. I'll leave him to you."

Hermann clicked his heels. He saluted and turned for the door.

"*Ja, mein Kommandant.*" He snapped at the two storm troopers, "Fall out the escort. Leave the prisoner."

A look of understanding passed between Ulrich von Kramer and his subordinate. Hermann stared contemptuously at the swaying figure; he hesitated, then hurried from the room.

Kramer was alone at last with his prisoner. He swore softly as he saw the American's knees buckle. The lanky body slumped silently to the floor, his arms spread-eagled before him.

Kramer cursed. There was no time to squander upon this unconscious fool. He moved to his desk and grabbed the carafe of water. He jabbed with his boot at the body on the floor. The man half-rolled on to his back. Kramer chuckled as he slowly trickled the water on to the swollen face. He stabbed again and again with the toe of his boot at the senseless swine.

"Get up, Yank," he blurted. "I can't waste time."

Then Jefferson stirred. He sat up, shook his head. His eyelids fluttered, then slowly opened. Kramer watched the man focusing upon his own face. He saw the fear, noticed the recoil from the nightmare of consciousness. (He'd have no trouble with this American now. Hermann had progressed ninety per cent of the way.) He kicked at the man's groin.

"Get up, I said."

Jefferson fumbled for the edge of the desk, hauled himself upright; he stood swaying, both hands on the desk for support.

Kramer grinned when he saw the mutilated fingertips. He had the American at his mercy now. Look, he was responding like a trained dog...

"Come to the window."

Jefferson lurched against the sill, clung, swayed — but remained on his feet. He was staring at Kramer.

"Wha' d'ya want?" His speech was slurred. Not surprising, Kramer thought, looking at the swollen, bruised face. There was hate burning in those brown eyes. "What' d'ya want, you lousy Kraut?"

That was better! The fool would understand now, maybe even respond. Kramer's arm shot out. He grasped the prisoner by the scruff of his sweater.

"Listen, Yank," Kramer said softly. He could feel his rage mounting. He felt himself trembling while he fought for control. "Listen to me carefully. Your life depends on it."

His prisoner was rational now, fully aware of his whereabouts.

"Go ahead," Jefferson said quietly. "You'll get nothing from me, Kramer."

He was standing upright now, his eyes bloodshot, his hands trembling by his sides as he struggled for self-control.

(*Most amusing, I must say*, Kramer admitted to himself. *I get a kick out of humiliating someone so cocksure.* There was that brat once, when he was at school…)

"Jefferson, for the last time: do you know what we're doing?"

Wearily the American shook his head.

"Nope."

"Have you informed your people of my whereabouts?"

"Aw, shut up, Kramer. Name, rank, number, that's all you'll get from me. Name, rank…"

Kramer's fist struck, smashing into the man's face. Jefferson reeled, took hold of himself, wiped the welling blood with the back of his hand.

"Stop playing the fool, Jefferson." Kramer was enjoying himself. But why did the fellow hold out? Pointless now. "Look out of that window, and listen to me."

He moved to a side window and threw it open. An icy blast cut across the room like a knife.

"D'you know where you are?"

139

The American was gasping in the rarefied air. He shook his head.

Kramer hesitated. He'd have to tell him now, at this last minute. Jefferson couldn't possibly escape. He might try, but if he did he wouldn't get far across those frozen wastes. Kramer walked to the window and pointed.

"Look, Jefferson. Look where you are — in the most remote corner of the globe. No one, except The Ring and the Greenland Conservatory Board, knows of the existence of this whaling station." He laughed as his arm swept across the window. "Look, man. Look at those buildings. What d'you think they are?"

Jefferson shrugged his shoulders.

"I'm taking you round them in a moment. I want you to be convinced about them, for, you see, Jefferson, they're to be our one link with the outside world, once the shooting starts. I'm sending you back to Europe on *Der Tag* plus three."

Jefferson was shaking his head. "What the devil are you blabbing about?"

Kramer hesitated, then took the plunge. "On D-Day, in eleven days' time, 28th June, to be precise," he began, "our Führer — we call him The Counsellor — starts the war." (*Ah! That's better. The Yank's taking notice now.*)

"See that tall building?" He pointed to the domed, concrete pile, emerging twenty feet above the rest of the station. "That disappears eighty metres underground. It holds three missiles."

Jefferson was peering through the windows now. From this control tower he could see round the whole horizon. The causeway of ice to the eastward, screening the whole base from seaward. The pool where the submarines not on patrol were secured. The buildings, dozens of flat-roofed sheds, nestling in their hidden valley. The ranks of cupola radar scanners, twisting and turning on their axes.

"Any aircraft passing overhead is immediately detected," Kramer continued. He was enjoying revealing their brainchild. "We get twelve minutes' notice at today's aircraft speeds. That gives us time to throw up *The Blanket*, as we call it. Watch."

He stepped to a control panel in the corner. He pushed a red button. He pointed out of the window. "Watch."

Nothing at first; then suddenly a wisp of white mist began wreathing the buildings. They watched it swirling like some monstrous reptile until, within seconds, the fog was swirling even around their watchtower.

"Not bad, Kramer."

The Kommandant pressed the black button. "It's simpler than you think: a network of pipes just below the ice. We switch on the current and the filament inside the pipe warms immediately. The sudden warmth meeting the cold air…"

The American was obviously impressed — look at him peering through the window now. He seemed completely absorbed by the buildings emerging as the fog subsided.

"Why the missiles?" the American asked quietly.

Kramer strolled to the wall map which stretched above the windows. He picked up the pointer and tapped the map. "New York is three thousand miles from here. In range of those."

He nodded towards the tallest building. He *was* enjoying himself. The American was shaking his head.

"On this side of the globe, we were forced to use rockets for the warheads. Then we realised the base could act in a dual capacity: it will be our Retreat while the thermo war is in progress. Here we can shelter while the West knocks hell out of the East. We'll be safe here, free from radiation hazards in our shelters while Russia retaliates on America and the West.

Don't you understand? In Germany, our planes are ready, armed with their rockets. They'll be loosed on Moscow at the identical moment that we launch our rockets here."

Jefferson was speechless. He slowly turned towards Kramer.

"You're mad," he whispered. "You're mad. You don't think we'll fall for this."

"There are *Russian* markings on some of those missiles. They are designed deliberately to misfire. At the identical moment, six supersonic fighter bombers will break away from NATO exercises in Western Germany. Each of these planes is manned by New Germans. Each aircraft is fitted with stand-off nuclear missiles. But" and Kramer nodded towards the tall buildings, "some will be duds, like those. They will have *American* markings on them."

Jefferson was looking intently at him, amazement in his eyes. "You're deliberately provoking a war between Russia and the States?" he whispered.

"That is so."

Jefferson gazed in silence across the barren snow plateau outside.

"And you and your Nazi friends," he said eventually. "You'll wait in safety here, while the holocaust burns itself out."

This was choice, very amusing. The Yank was quicker than he'd anticipated. "That's right, Yank."

"And when it's all over; when there's nothing left?"

Von Kramer's arm shot out. He twisted the American round to face him.

"Then the world's ours."

"What's left of it," Jefferson said.

"We've trained squads in every country throughout the world. On *Der Tag* they'll be first in the shelters. They'll emerge to take charge as soon as the worst of the radiation's over. See those?" He pointed to a cluster of lattice masts which the American had not seen. "They're extendable radio masts. With the power supplied by our nuclear submarines we can contact our *cadres* throughout the world. We're atom proof here."

Jefferson turned away, his face grey. He was staring blindly across the white roofs of this secret headquarters.

"D'you want to see for yourself, American?" Kramer snapped. "The power houses, the deep shelters, the control rooms. D'you want to see them, American? The missile gantries, the living quarters for the male and female staff. The New World will be peopled by pure Aryan stock, Yank."

Von Kramer was glorying in his exultation. The years of planning were finished. Action at last — in less than a fortnight ... he couldn't believe it. He felt carried away by his own words.

"Our New Germany will rule the new planet that rises from the ashes. By God, Jefferson! Nothing will stop us now. The twenty-eighth of June..." He smothered the emotion rising in his voice. "All these years we've sweated, toiled, my friend... Condemned at Nuremberg, hounded like vermin ever since; on the run, shunned, barred from any decent job. Yes, you blind fools..."

He was ice-cool in his suppressed rage. The American seemed terrified when he turned towards him.

"For years we've been planning this," he blurted. "The long years have passed now. Within a few days The Counsellor will take his rightful place here."

"Who's he?" Jefferson interrupted.

"Our new Führer. He's the leader of our New Germany. He will remain in Europe until its last moments. He leaves France by submarine for The Refuge in six days' time, as soon as I've reported that all is ready here. You see, I'm his Deputy." He was unable to conceal the pride in his voice. He paused, embarrassed.

"So you're all ready?" the American asked. "Quite prepared to murder the old order?"

"Yes. We wait only for *Der Tag* and The Counsellor's arrival. Once he has given the final order, nothing can halt events. At eleven o'clock, G.M.T., *Der Tag*, the rockets will be in the air. Five minutes later, Russia and America will be blasting each other and their allies to hell."

The American was speechless.

"Where do I come in, you maniac?" he blurted suddenly. "Why have you brought me here? Why have you kept me alive? You're not usually so considerate."

Kramer was enjoying this hugely. How the Yank wriggled!

"At first, when you recognised me, I thought that you might ignore the *rencontre*. When you picked up the scent, I feared you had stumbled upon something; cracked our security. If you had…" He paused and slid his finger across his throat. He grinned as the American turned again towards the window. "I realised you might have reported to your Security people. I had to know how much you knew, how much you'd reported."

Jefferson spun round. "You still don't know, Kramer," he said grimly. "But I can tell you this. You'll never get away with your crazy scheme. They're after you, bud."

Kramer laughed. The fellow was amusing, but futile.

"Of course." He was bored. "But I want to keep you alive a little longer. You'll be useful to us as a go-between should anything go wrong. We can always send you back to your masters to tell them we mean business. They might believe you."

"Why not now?"

"Idiot! You'd blow the secret of the dud missiles. The Big Boys might not go to war then, if they knew the missiles were 'planted'."

Kramer was growing impatient. If the schedule was not to be upset, he must *not* squander time. The Counsellor wouldn't like waiting for another batch of NATO manoeuvres.

"I can't waste more time on you, Yank," he said, picking up his cap. "I'm returning to Europe now to report to The Counsellor. He's a ruthless man, and I daren't keep him waiting. You'll try to escape, of course?"

He grinned down at the dejected figure. "I warn you, my sentries have orders to shoot on sight. It's very, very cold, very lonely out there. Over two hundred miles across the ice plateau to the nearest settlement… I wouldn't try it if I were you."

The American was leaping at him. He took him squarely on the chin.

"Guards!"

The door burst open and Hermann ran in towards them. The sentries were at his heels.

"Take him back to his cell, Hermann," Kramer commanded. "If I don't return on the twenty-third, switch off the heaters. Don't waste electric current on him. Let him freeze to death."

He took one last look at the pathetic American before he strode from the room.

"Goodbye, Yank," he chided. "What's it like to be the underdog?"

CHAPTER 15

The Pace Quickens

Kapitan-Leutnant Bernt Norden sighed with relief as he surfaced U-9 outside the ice barrier for the last time before returning to the Fatherland. Though he would have the Deputy Führer breathing down his neck for five days of the passage to St. Nazaire, he could even put up with Ulrich von Kramer for the hope of a couple of days in Berlin. These three months had been monotonous, but now there was frantic activity, judging by the comings and goings of V.I.P.s. *Der Tag* must be imminent. He'd be glad when it was all over: the sooner they could build the New Germany the better.

"Down periscope. Surface!"

He clambered up the tower, close on the heels of his signalman. This was a stupid time to enter *San Marco*, at the darkest period of the night, but who was he to remonstrate with that von Kramer? The man was too self-opinionated, too irascible for him, Bernt Norden, to cope with. And why did U-9 have to be chosen to take the Deputy Counsellor back to Europe?

He raised his binoculars as, mechanically, he drained the voicepipe. Ah! There was *San Marco*, her silhouette bold against the cliffs. Only one more docking before U-9 would be on her way at last. Would Marlene still be waiting for him? A pity he couldn't ask her to join The Ring. She would have made him a good wife. A pity, too, that her grandfather had been a Jew. It would have been fun...

"Coxswain closed up, sir."

He saw Klemming at the wheel beneath the bridge platform. A strange man his Coxswain, not as loyal as he would have liked.

"See *San Marco*?"

"*Ja, mein Kapitan.*"

"Steer for her."

"*Ja, mein Kapitan.*"

"Harbour stations. Cable party on the fore-casing."

He leant across the lip of the bridge. Strange business this: the tension was mounting, becoming intolerable. How much longer could the whole operation remain secret? Look at *San Marco* there, looming so close. Surely that enormous bulk would arouse suspicion in Hamburg? 'Jan Mittel Whaling Company.' Huh! Good cover, though...

"Steady as you go, Cox'n. Stop motor. I'll take her now."

"Very good, sir."

He coaxed her in towards the gantries standing sentinel at *San Marco*'s bows. He felt sorry for her crew: always at the beck and call of the submarines, day and night. When they weren't docking, they were storing.

"Starboard five. Slow ahead."

Just a touch should do it. He'd better warn the Deputy Counsellor they'd be secured in five minutes. Von Kramer was impatient to be on passage, Bernt Norden was certain of that. But he had to square-off his office aboard *San Marco* first; pick up his papers. A nuisance having to call at all; he had laid off the course for Jan Mayen island already.

"Stop motor. Tell the *Herr Deputy* that we shall be docking in five minutes."

"*Jawohl, mein Kapitan.*"

"Midships. Meet her... Steady."

Not bad... The for'd jumping-wire was lined up smack in the middle of *San Marco*'s bridge now. How easy it was — so silent, so efficient. U-9's bows were sliding beneath the gantries now. *San Marco* was asleep tonight.

"Call her up, Signalman," he ordered testily, "'bout time they showed up." He cupped his hands and yelled into the gloom of the floating dock.

"Stand by my lines!" He heard his words reverberating around the metal sides.

Someone shouted above him. The outline of a seaman stood silhouetted against the twilight, a heaving line coiled in his hands. The line was whistling through the air; it thudded upon the fore-casing. *San Marco*'s seamen were experts at mooring-up now.

He ducked instinctively as the gantry catwalk slid across his head. Two seamen stood there, checking his entry.

"Slow astern," he ordered down the voicepipe, and then he shouted over the bridge rail: "Out brows."

He felt the gentle tremble of U-9 as she went astern. As soon as she was secured he'd fetch the Deputy Counsellor himself. He'd better be certain that the brows were in position first, though! Ah! That was quicker ... there were lights twinkling in the bridge superstructure of *San Marco* now. The crane's jib lights were on too, throwing their shadows weirdly upon the scene.

"Stop motor." The dockside was stationary now. "I'm going below, Cox'n, to fetch The Deputy," he said, as he slipped down into the conning tower. "Man the side and tell the Officer of the Watch."

"*Jawohl, mein Kapitan.*"

The senior rating waited for him to pass, then the Cox'n was clambering through the hatch.

Norden found von Kramer waiting impatiently in the Ward Room. His aide (that snotty-nosed young puppy, Kurt Brandt) was standing obsequiously in the passage.

"We're getting out the brow now, *Herr Kommandant.*"

Von Kramer stood up, looking around the compartment. There was a long silence. What the devil was The Deputy up to now? It was incredible how he always had this terrifying effect on him, Bernt Norden, captain of one of New Germany's U-boats. The pause was so long that in the silence he could hear the cable party pattering on the fore-casing above their heads.

"Tell the men," the Deputy Counsellor said slowly, "that I like their boat. It's clean; it's efficient." He was looking through Kapitan-Leutnant Norden. "And tell them, *Kapitan,*" he went on, "that I'll be bringing back The Counsellor with me.

Von Kramer waited for the full effect of the news to sink in. "You have the honour of transporting him here from Europe."

The news stunned him for a moment. He'd really bought it then. He, Bernt Norden, had the responsibility for the safety of all their hopes. An honour maybe, but one he could well do without.

"Lead the way, Kapitan. I shan't be long in *San Marco.*"

Norden saluted, clicked his heels, then led the way towards the conning tower ladder.

"After you, *Herr Deputy.* My men will help you to the brow."

Von Kramer nodded, then walked briskly to the ladder to begin climbing the steel rungs. The aide pushed after his master. Norden swore softly.

"Warn the gangway staff," he whispered to his First Lieutenant as he went by. As he disappeared into the clammy tower, he saw Adolf Adler yanking the telephone from its bracket. At least there would be no mistake in etiquette. Kramer was a stickler for it.

At the top of the tower he had to wait a moment for Kramer's bulk to wriggle through the upper lid. The aide had scuttled after his master. He heard a brusque exchange on the bridge (Kramer couldn't do anything pleasantly); then he felt the cold lip of the upper hatch beneath his fingers. He hauled himself through, sick of the whole business. He'd have to hurry now to beat The Deputy to the gangway: he could slip down the other side of the bridge, if the aide didn't get in his way. Where was the fool?

He emerged through the hatchway, breathed the clean air. Someone was shutting the hatch behind him. What the devil was he playing at? It could be dangerous if they started the generators... He swung round angrily.

He was looking into the gleaming barrel of a heavy revolver.

"Silence," a voice snapped, in English.

As he leapt forwards, two arms were flung about him from behind, squeezing him like steel bands. Before he could open his mouth to shout, a wad had been jammed down his gullet. His feet slipped from under him. There was searing pain; his head was swimming. A blinding, whirling light and he knew no more.

They had taken Hank out for exercise at five in the morning. A guard in white furs had pounded on the door, drawn aside the bolts, then dragged him outside into the snow. Now the swine stood at the foot of the watchtower, his tommy gun at the ready, while Hank paced the snow.

"Twenty minutes, *du schweinhund.*"

Hank Jefferson, one-time Lieutenant U.S. Navy, found himself alone on the outskirts of the camp.

At first it had seemed cruelly cold. After the comparative warmth of his cell — a square box hewn from the ice wall surrounding the camp and heated by hot air — this raw cold cut through the inadequate dungarees he had been given on landing. A deliberate move to prevent his escape, he realised now.

Two hours out there on that windswept plateau, and he'd be as stiff as an icicle... He glanced at his watchdog, stuffed his hands in his pockets and turned his back. Blast the fellow. If he wanted to shoot him down in cold blood, through the back, let him! Hank had never in his life felt such misery.

His fingertips were still raw. The cold made them throb with pain, a pain that pumped through his whole system. These torturers were callous swine. His eyes roamed listlessly across the grey wastes. To the south, nothing but the vastness of a bleak whiteness: a terrifying solitude stretching into eternity. To the east, The Barrier, as they called it: that wall of ice separating this Nazi hideaway from the fjord outside. Then the cliffs on the south side of the uncharted fjord, blue with distance. The ice wall was so high that it screened *San Marco*'s masts. He gasped with amazement at the security of this hideaway. These Nazis were safe from discovery from all quarters. As far as Greenland realised, this was just another hunting station. The country must have renewed the licence automatically year after year. If any officious government inspector wished to investigate, he would have to give many weeks' notice. And this journey would take little to dissuade inspectors. They told him there had been only one. The unhappy man had been drowned on his journey back to civilisation, so they said...

Hank Jefferson swung round angrily. There was that accursed Refuge. There, those gigantic towers with the missile launchers. (Dammit, they were so cocky, so sure of themselves, these arrogant Huns. They'd even taken him last night to see the missiles before they flung him into his ice cell.)

He'd been convinced all right. He'd been numbed by the enormity of the crime. A hideous scheme — why, in their Teutonic thoroughness, they'd even shown him with pride the 'duds' with the U.S.S.R. markings upon their nosecones … trust the Nazis: only *they* could be so brutally callous.

Destroy civilisation so that Nazism might live — what a paradox. He flung round in disgust and looked again to seaward. Inside The Barrier was the harbour where the U-boats moored up after surfacing inside the Ice Wall. Perhaps *they* offered his only chance of escape?

Idly he allowed his gaze to wander over the black pool of water. Peter would have concentrated on that! But he, poor guy, even if he'd escaped a knife in his back after Hamburg, had obviously lost track. How the devil could he have followed *San Marco* so quickly, even if Admiralty had despatched *Rugged*? No, he, Hank Jefferson, was dead mutton — he might as well face it. How could he escape across *that* country… Ugh, he never did like the cold.

He turned to stare at his guard. The barrel of the gun was still facing this way. No, he couldn't run for the wastes — why die out there? He might as well give up.

There was nothing to do but pray. The first missiles would fly in less than a fortnight. Well, thank God he professed to be a Christian. Otherwise he'd cut his throat here and now.

"Fifteen minutes."

The guard's shout made him turn round. Hullo! Another U-boat had surfaced in the pool and was securing alongside. From here he could plainly see the figures on the bridge. There went the cable party, shoving the plank across. Reminded him of those first days in *Rugged* when first he'd met Peter…

The cluster of men was clambering ashore. He could see them stamping their feet in the snow. Even from here, he caught sight of the wisps of condensation from their breathing. Then they hustled off towards the entrance to the base. (Always in a hurry, these swine... Well, they hadn't much time now, had they? If they weren't ready now, after twenty years, they never would be.)

"Ten minutes."

Blast the guard. Why did he interrupt a guy's thoughts? *I'll go for a stroll, keep the muscles in trim. I must keep fit*, he thought; *I might get a chance, even yet. Even if they do kill me (that threat about switching off the heat wasn't funny — he'd no wish to freeze to death). Even if they kill me, by God, I'll take a few of 'em with me...*

He slapped his arms around and strode purposefully towards the distant ridge. He peered quickly over his shoulder: the bloodhound was following. He reached the rise when the guard bellowed across the snow: "Five minutes. *Kommen sie mit mir.*"

Hank turned round; spread his hands. The tommy gun's barrel swung towards him.

"Okay, Kraut. I'm coming."

He sauntered down the slope, tantalised by his inability to see across The Barrier. The U-boat was turning in her own length, whiteness frothing at her stern while she manoeuvred to face seawards.

He reached the guard, sauntered on slowly down the hill. Anyway, he'd enjoyed stretching his legs — at least they'd stopped torturing him. It was a miracle they'd tolerated him so long, these ruthless, callous devils... Hullo, what's this? A reception party?

A group of men was emerging from the exit through which he'd left The Refuge to take his exercise. One was a figure he dimly recognised from the past: a big man, with a huge barrel of a chest. He was slowly leading the way. Occasionally he looked backwards, while behind him came his advisers, close on his heels. Surely they couldn't be coming to interview him again? It couldn't be Kramer, could it? He'd left already — ah! The submarine, that explained it...

"*Wache, hierher!*"

Yes, that was the brute's voice all right. The guard had galvanised into action: he'd set the gun to safe and was scrambling through the snow towards the big man. He halted and raised his gun in salute. The party was close enough now for Hank to hear.

"Carry on inside, sentry."

Von Kramer spoke softly. The naval officers were crowding closely around him, their collars turned up against the cold. "Go and have your breakfast, guard. I want to talk to the prisoner. I will bring him in."

"*Jawohl, mein Kommandant.*"

"And give this letter at nine o'clock to the Duty Officer. Understand?"

"*Ja, Herr Kommandant.*"

The sentry saluted, then trudged off across the snow.

Von Kramer was walking slowly towards Hank. He looked pretty grim: there were circles beneath his cold eyes, and his cheeks were puffy. He was walking stiffly, and he was strangely silent. He stopped when they were three yards apart.

"Hank..."

He took no notice. His brain had been playing him tricks for days. He'd grown used to these cruel aberrations.

"Hank, keep calm..."

The voice came from behind the German leader; a muffled voice from one of the German N.C.O.s; a soft, English voice…

"Hank, for God's sake act normally. It's me — Peter."

Hank felt his knees buckling. His heart was pounding against his ribs. Then the man immediately behind Kramer, a slight figure in dark naval uniform, took a step aside.

Hank began to move forwards.

"Stay where you are, Hank."

Peter's eyes held him. *It was Peter Sinclair.* It must be. Too cruel a dream…

"Peter…" Hank heard the words whispering through his own lips. "What are you doing here, Pete? They got you too, bud?"

"We've come to get you, chum," the English voice drawled. "Do exactly as I say and we've got just the slimmest chance. Bungle it, and we're all lost… Now, Kramer, do as I say or I'll plug you dead."

The squat barrel of a Luger was sticking into Kramer's side. The German turned sharply and walked stiffly down the hill.

CHAPTER 16

Against the Odds

"Can you give us any more, Chief?"

Peter Sinclair looked up from the Ward Room settee at his Engineer Officer, that competent Scot. Craig shook his head.

"She's vibrating more than she should now, sir. The coolant is only just coping." The Chief rubbed his nose. "Five and a half days, you said, sir?"

Peter nodded.

"It's giving us thirty-five knots, Chief. We did it on trials." Craig smiled. "The weather was a bit different in Inchmarnock Water, sir."

"That's why I dived, Chief. Trimming's a bit dicey, isn't it?"

The Captain was smiling, but inside himself his nerves were on edge. Although he'd come farther east to avoid the pack ice and had kept the speed down until he was west of the northern tip of Spitzbergen, he did not like this: charging blindly through these waters at two hundred feet was still an unpleasant experience. They could, it was true, collide with some berg straying below the summer ice limit. Sonar was little use at this speed. He'd only dared dive yesterday, as soon as he got clear of the charted limit.

They'd been unlucky with the weather since they'd watched *San Marco* disappearing over the eastern horizon. He hoped Benson was coping all right. So long as he kept U-9's and *San Marco*'s crew firmly battened down in the fore-peak, he was safe. After scuttling U-9, Peter had given him all the hands he could spare from *Rugged*, including the Second Coxswain and

Hicks, the Stoker P.O. *Rugged* was dangerously short of hands, particularly at this speed. Taggart was coping adequately as First Lieutenant, but thank goodness he'd kept Withers, the Coxswain. At this speed no one else could match the older man on the afterplanes, but the Coxswain was tiring under the strain.

Peter looked up. The Chief had gone. Everyone was pushed to their limit, with one object in view: could they coax this nuclear machine to reach the Toulon area in time? This was the sixty-four-thousand-dollar question: upon the answer balanced the fate of future generations.

Peter wiped his hand across his face. It was sticky with sweat, but not only from the heat. The realisation of the terror he was up against was having its effect.

He looked across at the tall figure sprawled in the bunk opposite. Hank was out to the wide. He'd been asleep now for eighteen hours: they must have given him hell. Look at the poor chap's nails — a mangled mess under those bandages. Those savage brutes... Peter gritted his teeth. This was the barbarity, this the inhumanity that threatened the world.

He rose quietly from the settee. He couldn't settle down with *Rugged* porpoising like this. He had no wish, though, to undermine his officers — they were doing pretty well, considering. Take Brock there, leaning over the chart table. When he wasn't in the motor room he was checking O'Donovan's navigation, since Taggart had become Acting First Lieutenant. There had been no distinctions of seniority: it had been the most suitable man for each duty.

His eyes wandered round the Control Room. She was waltzing between one hundred and ninety and two hundred and ten feet (you couldn't expect much else at this speed). Taggart was standing astride between the gauges, watching the trim. Withers sat motionless, eyes glued on the bubble. Thank God for that dependable, competent man…

Peter was worried. He'd extricated *Rugged* from the ice safely and *San Marco* must be safely on her way by now. Yet, though *Rugged* was happily set on her south-westerly course now, what next? She'd be clearing Jan Mayen island to starboard shortly after dark; tomorrow, on the evening of June twenty-second, she'd be between the Faeroes and the Hebrides. Where then, for crying out loud?

In Greenland, the compulsion was to escape: the fate of the world was of secondary importance. Now, the crushing responsibility lying on his shoulders was too much: particularly as Peter was groping now, uncertain where to go, what to do.

Ulrich von Kramer had refused to talk. The only information he'd let slip, apart from what he'd told Hank, was that they'd be too late, whatever they did. *Der Tag* was on June 28th. The wheels were in motion, nothing, nobody could halt the process of time.

Peter had interrogated the two prisoners separately, on passage through the pack ice, during that nerve-racking period at slow speed. With Taggart and Withers as witnesses in the Ward Room, he'd grilled Kramer first — without a glimmer of success. The pink-faced Nazi had leered and become offensive, entirely confident in his own immunity and the inevitability of events now in train. Should Kramer even lose his life, nothing could now halt the crisis. Though Kramer now regretted his indiscretion in boasting to Hank back at the base, he knew the error could not affect the outcome. Peter was beaten. He sent Kramer back to the fore-ends, under the guard of Able Seaman Hawkins.

U~9's captain had been incarcerated in the after-ends. Though his interrogation had been carried out under the same conditions, he was a different customer from the Deputy Counsellor.

"Name?" snapped Peter, remaining seated on the Ward Room settee.

"Norden. *Kapitan-leutnant.* Three-nine-two-four-o."

Peter couldn't prevent the smile twitching at the corners of his mouth.

"You are well trained, *Herr Kapitan.*"

"*Jawohl,*" the U-boat C.O. said softly.

Peter recognised the Bavarian dialect: not so ugly as the north-German. The man was not so truculent as his master.

"We are trained too, *Kommandant,*" Peter said, proffering a cigarette. "Only name, rank and number." He smiled up at the brown eyes looking down at him. Norden must be about the same age. The German took the cigarette.

"Submariners are the same," Peter said, "the world over."

Taggart stood aside. Norden's mouth twitched into a smile as he sat down opposite the Captain.

"We have the same job to do," Norden said.

An unusual face, Peter thought. *Sensitive but strong. Why had he allowed himself to be duped? A Nazi? Amazing...* Perhaps if Peter accepted him into Ward Room life the fellow might give something away...

"Get out the poker dice, Number One," he said in English, looking up at Taggart. "Let's roll dem bones." He winked deliberately at his officers. He turned again to the Hun.

"Can you speak English?" he asked in German.

"A leetle." Norden was smiling.

It was certainly true that submariners are the same breed in any country. The Yanks had a similar outlook; now Norden was picking up the thread of 'liar dice' as easily as if he'd been born a Briton.

"Can the *Herr Deputy* play this game?" Peter asked, his eyes fixed on the ivory cubes on the table.

"No."

Norden snapped the word. He seemed irritated at the mention of von Kramer's title.

"Probably hasn't had much practice," Peter said, throwing a fourth King. "Takes skill."

"And courage..." the Hun said, looking up. Then he bit his lip.

"I thought he'd plenty of guts," Peter replied. Norden disliked his boss.

"Ashore he's all right, *Herr Kapitan*," the U-boat C.O. said, his eyes contemptuous, his lower lip jutting. "But here..." He shrugged his shoulders and laughed harshly. "He lives in our Ward Rooms all the time on passage — claustrophobia." The man raised his eyebrows and spread his hands. "Embarrassing, you understand."

"What did you give me, Number One? A Queen *and* a Jack?" Peter picked up the Knave, shook the dice and threw it open.

Norden laughed when the ten came up. "How you say? Not good luck, eh?"

Ten minutes later Peter dismissed the U-boat captain. He sent for the Chief and the Coxswain.

"Now we're all here," he began, "I've had an idea. We've *got* to make Kramer tell us where his boss hangs out. All we know is that it's somewhere in France — he told Lieutenant Jefferson that. If we can't make the swine talk, we might as well pack up."

"Ditto the world," Taggart murmured.

"*We're forced to make him talk*. That supercilious face conceals all we've got to know."

"I could smash it in for him," Withers whispered.

"No good, Cox'n. He's used to that treatment: he's an expert at dishing it out himself." Peter leant forward. His words were low and precise: "I've an idea. Remember our visit to Newport News when we refuelled?"

Taggart nodded.

"Remember that humiliating afternoon when the U.S.A.A.F. took us up for a flight?"

The Coxswain was grinning, the crow's feet at the corners of his eyes crinkled in amusement. "They gave you the works, sir."

Ewan Craig's soft Scottish sing-song chipped in: "Seem to remember oor gettin' oor ain back."

Peter glanced at his fellow conspirators.

"That's just what we're going to do now." He smiled but his grey eyes were hard. "It may be unethical, but it's our only chance. Kramer's got to crack. Norden says he's claustrophobic. We'll see if he's right. Chain Kramer down in the for'd pump-space, Coxswain. Fetch him now."

The Chief was donning his leather gloves. "Shall I get weaving, sir. Same as last time?"

Peter nodded, then turned to Taggart. "Ease her down gently, Number One, to three knots. I'll take her down slowly to eight hundred feet. We should bottom shortly after, if our charts are right."

Peter shook his head.

"I've got to see Kramer first. I'll give the orders."

The Deputy Counsellor, *Herr Kommandant* Ulrich von Kramer, Iron Cross-with-Oak Leaves, fumed with humiliation. Livid with rage, yes, but, by God, he'd won. That Sinclair had *not* got the better of him. He, Kramer, had won this second round, just as he would win the world title. He'd never squeal.

Everything was at stake.

"Get going."

A sailor's voice growled behind him. This was that English seaman who'd been watching him like a bloodhound. Kramer turned slowly back into the passage. He'd take his time for these *schweinhunds*...

The barrel of a pistol was pressing into the small of his back. He quickened his pace. (He had a nasty feeling this blue-eyed seaman with the boxer's build was itching to pull that trigger.) Sinclair had tried terror to make him talk. How had the fellow discovered the chink in his armour? Being cooped up by himself was the one terror that had haunted him in these horrible submarines. Why the devil were the Englishmen locking him up in solitary confinement?

Kra-a-a... Kra-a-a... Kra-a-a...

He jumped as the emergency change-of-depth klaxon blared in his ear. His heart was banging against his ribs. What the devil was wrong? Look, they were slamming shut those huge steel doors.

"*Pronto*," the seaman behind him snapped. Kramer forced himself onwards. A man held the steel door for an instant. His face was taut.

"Quick!" He stood with legs astride to control the massive bulkhead.

Kramer felt the deck sliding away from under his feet. He heard that sailor, Hawkins, cursing behind him as they slithered feet-first through the small opening. Kramer was sweating when he reached the fore-ends. The main lighting dimmed, suddenly went out. In the blackness, he could pick out the luminous figures of a dial. A green pointer was creeping slowly round it.

"What's happening?" he shouted.

"Shut up. We're going deep. We're out of control."

"*Out of control...?*"

The emergency lights came on. A pale light spread weirdly through the compartment. The machinery gleamed in the shadows.

"Come on — get going."

Kramer looked round wildly. Where was he being taken?

"Get below," Hawkins growled.

A rectangle of light opened at Kramer's feet. A short ladder led down from it. He resisted the pressure in the small of his back.

"Down there?" he whispered.

"That's what the Captain said."

The barrel dug viciously. "Get on down!" the sailor growled.

Kramer swore beneath his breath. He loosened the collar of his tunic. He had begun to sweat as the first wave of nausea swept through him. He closed his eyes an instant, shook his head. He turned then towards the bulkhead; he grabbed the handrail. He was mesmerised by his own clambering down the ladder into the pump-space.

When he reached the bottom he could not stand erect. The compartment must have been no more than a metre and a half high. It was a steel cube of about nine metres, most of the space being taken up by a huge rectangular box, studded by valves on their spindles. He kept one hand on this chunk of machinery, then squatted on his haunches. His left hand brushed something greasy: a camp stool. *I shan't be too uncomfortable*, he thought. *Once I get used to this, I'll be all right. Sinclair won't win. To hell with Sinclair...*

His eyes slowly became accustomed to the gloom. A mass of machinery with a gauge sticking up at eye level on the frame of the pressure hull. He found his eyes drawn to this yellow luminosity of the depth gauge with its pointer. It was creeping round the dial now...

"You 'appy?"

He looked upwards towards the voice. A head had appeared upside down and was peering through the hatch. It had blue eyes and belonged to the seaman, Hawkins.

"*Schweinhund!*"

He spat the word. He'd stick this out. His voice remained steady, though he was fighting off a prickliness at the back of his neck.

"I'm up 'ere, if yer changes yer bleedin' mind..."

Kramer understood the observation. But the seaman could wait there till eternity.

Ulrich von Kramer was not afraid of an absurd thing like this. He'd suffered from claustrophobia, yes, of course he had. But only once, badly. That germ of panic, deep inside him — he must smother it now, before it grew into something monstrous. But what was there to worry about? They weren't being hunted and depth-charged. There was nothing to do but sit here and wait. Perhaps he'd wreck the boat and take them all with him? He stared at the box of tricks in front of him. A warning in red letters was engraved on a tally immediately below the gauge:

DANGER: CHECK EACH INLET VALVE SHUT
BEFORE OPENING OUTLETS

Some of these valves must open directly to the sea. *Verflucht!* The sea was only held back by this steel plate. He lifted his hand and gently nibbed his finger along the rough, cork-pointed side. He held up his finger and saw the droplets. It must be moist down here.

The pale light snicked out as a bright lamp came on in the corner. At least those in the Control Room should be able to see now. What had gone wrong? The boat still felt bow-down. He glanced at the gauge. Himmel! It was racing round the dial. Three hundred feet.

He tried to push the terror from him. Why had they shut all the watertight doors so swiftly? An emergency: hadn't that sailor said so? He stared at the depth gauge. Why, for God's sake, were these English so individualistic? What was wrong with metres? A metre was (what was it?) about three feet. The pointer was creeping up to a red mark on the dial. He leaned forward to read the small letters printed alongside this danger line.

TESTED SAFE DIVING LIMIT

The red mark was at six hundred feet — at least just above it — about six hundred and fifteen. He tried to repel the fear that was gnawing insistently in his mind. Disregard the fear, kill it... What was six hundred and fifteen feet?

Ah, easy! One hundred metres; didn't seem far on land. But down here, with these depths hungry to crush the life out of them — so near... He turned his face from the curvature of the pressure hull.

A telephone shrilled suddenly from above. He jumped; felt his heart hammering. There was a thump in the compartment above.

"We're opening up from collision stations," a cheerful voice sang down sarcastically through the hatch: "Captain says you're not to worry. Everything's all right."

Why did they treat him like a child? Why try to hide things from him? Surely the submarine shouldn't be as deep as this? Look, six hundred feet and still going down. Panic was gripping him; the pointer crept round the dial ... it was crossing the danger mark of the tested safe diving depth.

Well, Sinclair must know what he was doing. He'd been in submarines long enough. Accidents *did* happen in submarines, however, even in peacetime. Why, at The Refuge, one U-boat had failed to return from patrol last year. Ice, they'd said...

He took a grip on himself. *This, Kramer, was no way to behave.* He'd try to sit still for five minutes. He'd fix his thoughts on *Der Tag*, force his mind from the terror.

Would The Counsellor be closing down yet? Probably. It was the twentieth of June today — or was it? Difficult to tell in this tin can. (He was afraid, he had to confess it. Look at that damned gauge: the pointer was still crawling deeper. Nearly seven hundred feet...)

Seven hundred ... the limit was *six*. (*Had they noticed it? The English are so casual compared to we Germans. I'll tell the sentry, just in case...*) He sat upright, gripped the piping leading into the valve box.

No, wait a bit. They'll think I'm scared... Hold on. I'll yell at eight hundred. Mustn't look at the gauge. He wrenched his eyes away from the luminous figures. *Concentrate, Ulrich, concentrate upon Der Tag...*

But what was fifteen metres? If he could get that, he'd calculate the safe depth. He'd reached one hundred metres — six hundred feet. *Fifteen was one-five divided by* ('over' wasn't it?)... *Wish I'd worked harder at school. Long ago now. Things were different in those days.* He could remember his father coming home from the front in 1915. Blinded. Groping his way into the dingy living room of what they called their home; led by a woman ambulance driver; feeling for the forgotten objects, his hands outstretched, dirty bandages swathing his eyes ... long time... *Three metres — no, five. Five, that was it...*

Now there was an ache, just below his heart. He could feel it if he pressed with his hand. *Good God, was he getting a heart attack? Men of his age did. Terror the cause, they would say. Fear triggered some gland which stimulated the heart and made it race. Couldn't cope. Phut! just like that — gone. Stiff all of a sudden.* Rigor mortis. He couldn't deny the terror now ... it was with him now, deep, deep inside, and swelling like a monstrous growth.

His eyes had strayed back to the gauge. He snatched a peep ... eight hundred and *sixty* feet. *Donnerwetter!*

He hurled himself towards the hatchway. His feet felt rooted to the oily deck.

"Guard! Guard!"

His words rang, a hollow sound against the steel.

"Guard!"

More urgent now. He recognised the hysteria in his voice.

Suddenly a grinning face appeared above him. The mouth opened grotesquely.

"'Ullo!"

Kramer pointed to the gauge. He opened his mouth, but no sound came. He tried again, croaking brokenly: "Nine hundred feet," he whispered.

The pink face above grinned obscenely. "Can't do much abaht it, mate."

"Safe limit," Kramer whispered, "is six hundred."

His words tailed off. He could feel the sailor mocking him. He didn't care now: the Kapitan must be told, must, *must,* MUST...

"'s right."

"The Kapitan knows?"

"Should 'ope so. 'E's doing 'is best. Bit o' trouble with the 'planes. Boat's out o' control."

Kramer felt the colour draining from his face. These insane English...

"Yeah. Can't do nuffink abaht it," said the seaman as he sipped a tea mug. "Leave it to the Captain, mate." He was grinning. "Never been so deep as this, though."

The klaxon blared again. Kramer felt the wetness of the tea as it slopped down upon him. The seaman leapt backwards, springing for the watertight door. At the same moment, Kramer felt the bows falling away steeply beneath his feet.

Good God! She was plunging even deeper. He staggered backwards and threw out his hands to save himself.

The main lighting flickered, went out. The hatch cover banged down on to the hatch coaming. He saw the clips twisting and locking it shut, clips turned by the seaman above. He was a prisoner, locked alive by himself in his steel coffin.

In this stygian darkness he crouched like an animal, staring at the yellow-green figures on the dial in the corner. Through the red mist that was swimming before his eyes, he saw nothing but the pointer. A luminous tell-tale creeping towards a terrible death ... nine-fifty and then (he thought he could hear the faint tick!) the pointer was hard against the stop. Over one thousand feet...

At this angle he could not regain the stool. He was flung to the far end, where he sprawled along the deck. He could still pick out the luminous glow of the gauge from here.

Then he felt it... He held his breath. Yes, there it was again. He was tilting his head, he knew, even in this blackness. A rumble, a distinct rumble; beneath his feet at first, then increasing suddenly all around him, a trembling of the boat's structure. The whole machine was disintegrating; he grabbed a steel pipe and in his agony started wrenching at it.

He could hear faint shouting: must come through the hatch. Someone in authority... Yes, there it was again ... he could make it out, now that the rumbling had stopped. He dragged himself frantically towards the hatch. He heard the shriek of the telephone buzzer. The muffled words were all too plain: "Water coming in through the bow-caps!"

God, oh God! He jerked his head at the gauge. Stuck at a thousand feet... "I mustn't panic. Ulrich, Ulrich..."

He knew he was screaming to himself. The hysteria was gripping him, toppling the last vestiges of control. The miasma was choking him. The monster had him now by both hands — it was at his throat, groping, throttling...

And then, above his shouting, he heard it ... a high-pitched screech, scrabbling along the steel plating by his head. Metal being torn apart, screeching ... then, silence.

With terrifying suddenness, no sound ... a drip of water; drip ... drip ... then a trickle, spattering in the bilges. Splashing now, growing to a deluge...

"I can't stand it," he was sobbing. "I can't... I can't."

He took the gauge between his hands. He squeezed it with all his strength. There was a voice somewhere, shouting, yelling. He heaved and wrenched, shaking the gauge insanely. Wild cries they were now distant, animal noises.

"I'll finish you, I'll kill you. Kill, kill, kill..." He could not hear his screams. "Let me out, let me out; *for God's sake, let me out!*"

He was holding his head between his hands. Pressing the temples, smothering the pain. He jumped up. He started banging against the hatch cover. Bang! bang! "Let me out, let me out..."

The blackness had him now, enveloping, throttling. Blue waves swept over him; there were crimson clouds, flashes of light. The water was a torrent now — he could hear it cascading and swirling beneath his feet. Seawater — chlorine...

"For God's sake…" He was battering feebly now, blubbing like a child. He knew no shame for the tears streaming down his face. "Help, help! Help! Help, help…!" His fists were pulp. He recognised dimly that the wetness was blood. He cared not. He must get away from this crushing, overpowering terror. The boat was caving in … it was gyrating round now, on its beam ends.

There was a roaring in his ears; the world was spinning round him. Then, suddenly, a flash of light blinded him from above.

CHAPTER 17

Cap Benat

Peter Sinclair stood in front of the small mirror in his cabin: clean-shaven after an hour's scraping in the basin, he wore a tropical suit of fawn twill, and a dark blue tie with horizontal white stripes. He could pass as a Frenchman if the cut of his jacket had not been disturbed by the holster beneath it. He preferred the comfort of the Colt .45 to sartorial excellence. He could have looked worse after the strain of the last few days. June the nineteenth had been the worst: *everything* had depended upon Kramer cracking. And the Deputy *had* cracked — completely. (The air pressure on the gauges had worked better than Peter had expected.) Kramer's abject squealing had been nauseating: he would have done literally anything to avoid being returned to the claustrophobic pump-space. His interrogators, Peter and Hank, had been merciless: they had extracted every scrap of information.

After the grilling, Peter had summoned his senior men. They had been grim, nearly inarticulate with the gravity of the situation. With the W/T set out of action and the aerial smashed by the pack ice, they were cut off from Admiralty. Kramer did not realise this. To a man, Peter's council of war that assembled in the Ward Room had agreed on action of their own choosing: there was little choice.

Peter glanced at the clock above his cabin door. Eleven forty-five; surfacing as soon as the folboat was ready. He brushed his hair. He was taking a risk, leaving the boat under Taggart's command. Peter had written out concise orders:

when the folboat had shoved off for the second time with the last passengers, *Rugged* was to dive. The shore party would be landing on Cap Benat. There was no time for fancy waistcoats. Anyway, The Counsellor could not know of their intended landing. Kramer's letter would have allayed any suspicions in the minds of those in The Refuge.

Once Kramer had divulged the whereabouts of The Counsellor's H.Q. and his timetable, matters had simplified. *Rugged*'s reactor had behaved itself: for six days now she had proceeded at one hundred feet at thirty-five knots. Apart from the momentary failure of the coolant on the first day, the twentieth, west of Spitzbergen, the boat had behaved magnificently. North-east of Iceland on the twenty-first of June, between the Faeroes and the Hebrides on the twenty-second; south-west of Ireland on the twenty-third, and on the twenty-fourth, tropical rig for the troops as Finisterre came up on the dawn search. Cape St. Vincent at noon, brown and shimmering with heat-haze, then The Straits at sunset. The Rock of Gibraltar crouching to the northward: he took *Rugged* deliberately towards the Moroccan coast. (He had no wish to run foul of British destroyers at this moment.)

It had blown hard all yesterday, the twenty-fifth, as *Rugged* slipped past the Balearics and across the Gulf of Lyons. Their landfall on Cape Sicie at sunset had been bang on the knob: the flashing light, marking the approaches to the French naval port of Toulon, had seemed very close. He had threaded *Rugged* between the Iles d'Hyères, and now she lay at periscope depth, less than a mile from that dark and forbidding Cap Benat.

Since Kramer had capitulated, there were moments when Peter felt almost fond of him. The information that had streamed from his lips had gushed like a torrent. His terror of further confinement had destroyed his will.

It was the ingenuity of this mysterious Counsellor which astounded Peter. By fashioning a villa on the Côte d'Azur into his headquarters, The Counsellor was above suspicion. Why, even an ex-President lived here... With short-wave transmitters sited on the small private island which was connected by a causeway to the villa, The Counsellor could direct his forces in Europe at will.

Decentralisation throughout Europe, particularly in Germany, was his policy. No top Nazi knew the identity of his fellow conspirators; each Group Controller was separated; in the final countdown on *Der Tag*, each of those seven Nazi pilots in the West German wing of the NATO Strike Force knew not whom his fellow conspirators might be. That was the plan.

The organisation was so decentralised, so vast that it was impossible to destroy it should someone accidentally blunder upon its existence.

It was the twenty-sixth of June in another quarter of an hour. Forty-eight hours later, it would be *Der Tag* — the day of reckoning for the whole world.

The band of men around *Rugged's* Ward Room table knew that upon them rested the final outcome. There was not even time to telephone Joe Croxton in London. Better, first, to cripple The Counsellor and his brainchild at Cap Benat. That would postpone *Der Tag*, surely? They could get in touch with Admiralty afterwards. Better to smother the monster at birth than risk those six planes taking off from that West German airfield in two dawns' time.

Peter gritted his teeth: there was no other course open to him. He picked up his battered panama hat and climbed down into the Control Room.

"Folboat and shore party ready, sir." Taggart saluted. "Ready to surface, sir."

Peter doffed his hat and glanced round the Control Room he might never see again. It was suddenly very quiet. Only the whine of the motor, the chuckle of the telemotor system. He met the eyes of his men. He turned suddenly towards the periscope and snapped his fingers. The steel tube slid upwards.

It was, mercifully, very dark up top. Black as pitch — through this lens he couldn't distinguish the horizon. Ah! There was the fixed red light upon the hill. Cap Benat light, the chart read, four hundred feet high, standing back from the Cap, and on high ground. He felt his heartbeats pounding against his eardrums. He smiled to himself: he hoped Kramer, standing by the fore-hatch in the gloom of the red lighting in the fore-ends, was feeling worse than he was. No turning back now. He swallowed and slammed shut the handles. He glanced at the clock: 0340. It would soon be dawn.

"Surface," he snapped.

Hank Jefferson and Bill Hawkins had landed first to reconnoitre. Their 'O.K.' on the infrared lamp invited Peter and his important passenger to follow. Then out of the darkness, the folboat bumped alongside. From the fin, Peter watched Kramer step gingerly into the bobbing canoe. He heard the plop of the discarded steadying lines. Hawkins was away into the darkness with his charge: if Kramer played funny beggars now that they were entering the lion's den, they were finished...

"So long, Number One."

Peter climbed down the ladder inside the fin and emerged through the door on to the casing. He tiptoed across the steel plating which was awash. His eyes were accommodated now to the darkness.

The rocky coast seemed very close. He could smell the resin of the pines on the offshore breeze, see the ribbon of breakers swirling lazily against the rocks. Behind him, on the horizon, lights twinkled on the island of Porquerolles. To the east, Port-Cros and the Ile du Levant, their outlines silhouetted against the night sky. These few minutes of waiting were gruelling: his career, his life, the fate of millions hung upon his correct appraisal of the situation. A moment's weakness and all was lost. There was a thud at his feet. The blackened face of Able Seaman Hawkins was peering up at him from the darkness.

"Right, sir."

Peter waited for the swell, then nipped into the bobbing folboat. He took the for'd position, shoved off with his paddle. He heard the rumble of *Rugged* going astern. He glanced over his shoulder. How rapidly she was sliding into the obscurity of the night! He raised his paddle above his head while he listened. Then in the darkness behind him he heard her main vents opening, the roar of escaping air.

They were on their own now. He dug his paddle into the water. Hawkins knew where to land; leave the steering to him.

Right ahead was the Cap: a shoulder running into the sea. There was some sort of fortification on its crest, like those old Saracen forts that had been fortified by the Germans during the Occupation. Hawkins turned the canoe to starboard and allowed the promontory to pass down their port side. As they rounded the point, the mainland came up right ahead. Then, in the pines, he distinguished the outline of a large villa. As the canoe drove inshore, Peter caught sight of the causeway connecting the point to the mainland. The concrete mass towered high above them. (Lucky they'd decided to enter the villa by the conventional route of the main road. Brazen bluff seemed the only chance...)

A half-moon of white sand opened up on their port bow. Peter laid his paddle along the canvas and allowed Hank to guide her in. He felt fear breathing down his neck. The pines were black, evil sentinels leering down expectantly upon them. Were they walking into a trap, perhaps? He pushed away the thought and shivered as the forefoot of the canoe scraped along the sand. From the shadows emerged two men, one close behind the other.

Peter heard Bill Hawkins splashing behind him. Two strong arms helped him from the canoe. He'd not even wet his shoes.

"Thanks, Hawkins."

"Part of the 'awkins service, as you might say, sir."

Peter glanced at the cliffs above them.

"If we're not here by dawn," he whispered, "get back to *Rugged*. Secure the folboat here, ready for crash launching. We're entering that villa by the front door."

He looked at Kramer. There was a change in the man already: he was squaring his shoulders with his usual arrogance.

"Get cracking, Hank. Watch the blighter." He drew his Colt and turned towards von Kramer. "If we're discovered, you're the first to die. Understand?"

"You won't get away with this, Sinclair. The Counsellor'll have you for mincemeat."

Peter turned to his seaman. "So long, Bill."

The man's head nodded in the darkness. Then suddenly he took Peter's hand.

It was a dark night. The stars were dancing in a cloudless sky and to seaward, their reflections, like pale fingers, gleamed on the mirror-surface. Ahead lay the cliff, topped by the stunted pines.

Hank was moving like a shadow, Kramer next, Peter bringing up the rear. He cocked his Colt and let Kramer feel its muzzle in the small of his back. The German moved as silently as his escort. By his movements, he'd been trained in Commando warfare.

The cliff was not difficult, but the spines of the prickly scrub tore at their clothes. Then they were on the clifftop, the sea breaking lazily against the rocks one hundred feet below.

No sign of *Rugged* to seaward. The red light of Cap Benat's lighthouse gleamed far above them on the pine-clad hill. And ahead, deep in those pines, he could see already the outline of the villa.

What a superb hideaway! The Counsellor was no fool. This headland was studded with similar properties. Peter could see their outlines among the pines which mantled the headland stretching into the Mediterranean. The private beaches nestled among the little coves fringing the Cote d'Azur. This villa was one of many but was more secluded by being at the extremity of the Cap.

They had stumbled upon a track and this was leading across the shoulder of the point. Then they were in the pines, and the air was soft with the tang of resin. The scent was nostalgic, reminding him of the cedars in Bermuda. His thoughts were wandering, but he was jerked suddenly to an awareness of his danger. He had bumped into Kramer: Hank must have halted. Peter's skin prickled along the back of his neck when he heard the weird sound.

A hound was baying in the pines. Another brute took up the savage howl, then pandemonium broke loose. Peter heard the animals tugging at their chains. A light came on in the trees above them. Suddenly it was as bright as day.

Hank did not hesitate. He stepped from the trees and on to the drive stretching before him to the villa's entrance. He turned towards Peter and yelled in German at the top of his voice: "What a welcome, *Herr Deputy*! Is this the way they greet you?" The Yank grabbed Kramer. The German stumbled on to the drive. "Speak, you lousy Kraut," Hank hissed, his eyes everywhere. "We're being watched, Pete. I'll bet they've mikes in the trees."

Peter dug his pistol into Kramer's back and the result was dramatic. The German yelled towards the closed gates of the forecourt: "Call off your confounded dogs. This is the Deputy Counsellor, you idiots."

At this hour of the night, though the lights of the villa were still burning, his words rang hollowly through the pines. A bad dream. Peter gripped the Colt for reassurance.

When the pandemonium had subsided, Peter heard a click above him in the pines. There was a crackle in the branches and a voice announced in German: "Welcome, Deputy. We're expecting you."

The loudspeaker snicked, went dead. Peter was shaken by the suddenness of events. Had their approach been observed, from the landing onwards? Maybe they'd had lookouts on the islet that was connected to the causeway?

This was the moment for decision: go in and take the consequences. Turn and run — find the first telephone and tip off Joe Croxton in London? He hesitated. Hank had turned towards him, waiting for the next move. Peter's heart was bumping against his ribs. Go back, turn now, while there was still time. Grab the sensible way out. A breath of suspicion was needling him: *Watch out, boy — watch out...*

He was nodding at Hank when the decision was taken from him. Kramer bellowed through the pines: "Open up! We're coming in."

Hank fell back and strode on the right of their prisoner. Peter slipped the gun and his hand into his jacket pocket. His thumb protruded and upon it he hung his hat. The bulge of the pistol was invisible, yet Kramer felt its persuasion as they walked towards the gatehouse. Another light came on. As they scrunched on the gravel, the gates swung open silently. (Photo-electric cell, probably.) Peter dropped half a pace behind their hostage.

"You know what to do, Kramer," he whispered. "One slip and I pull this trigger."

He could hear the German's rapid breathing. Under these bright arc lights he could see the tiny beads of perspiration mottling Kramer's forehead. The man's head was twisting nervously from side to side.

They were reaching the massive front doors now. A sweet-smelling daphne fringed the entrance. A dark-suited flunkey stood between the doors, while two men held them open. The flunkey clicked his heels, gave the Nazi salute.

"Franz," Kramer grunted. "Take me to The Counsellor."

Their footsteps echoed from the marble of the spacious hall. Franz led them to the far side. He held open two further doors. Kramer hesitated. He glanced at Franz. Peter held his breath, crooked his finger round the trigger... What had passed between the two?

"After you, *Herr Deputy.*"

Was Peter mistaken, or was there an undertone of triumph in Franz's words? Terrifying. They'd walked straight into the trap. Thank God for Taggart out there. No news within six hours and he was to proceed to Toulon and contact Admiralty. That would still allow time to arrest the catastrophe — if Admiralty acted, if Admiralty were convinced. If, if… Better to fix this fanatical Counsellor at source. Where *was* this fellow, Franz, shoving them now? Peter followed Kramer through the double doors; he heard the click when they closed behind them.

They were in a large, open room. There were no windows, but only one domed skylight, high in the ceiling, and no pictures on the buff walls; no womanly touch here, except for the soft carpet under their feet. At one end stood a large executive-type desk. At the back of this ran the far wall, the only lighted feature in the room. It was blue-green and across this were swimming the fish of a tropical aquaria. The whole wall glowed with a diffused light hidden at its foot: probably an optical effect, the image being reflected on to this wall which served as a screen. The result was very beautiful. And in front of them, behind the desk, sat a bald-headed man — motionless, eyeing them.

Kramer stopped suddenly. He had halted in his tracks as if he hadn't expected to meet The Counsellor face to face.

"Good evening, Ulrich."

In the shock of the moment, Peter glanced at Kramer. The colour had drained from his face. The eyes stared, the lips were slack. The man was mesmerised, like a rabbit by a weasel. In the silence Peter heard the click of the Deputy's heels.

"It is good to see you, *mein Herr.*" Kramer's voice sounded surprised, servile.

"You are early, *Herr Deputy*," the man purred from behind the desk. "And who are your friends?" The putty face peered inscrutably at Hank, before turning to Peter. The eyes beneath the bald pate were brittle, as cold as a fish's. Peter shivered.

"My guards?" Kramer asked quietly. "They've escorted me across France."

Peter nodded imperceptibly at Hank. A look of understanding passed between them. Hank'd take the man at the desk — Peter, Franz and Kramer. One bullet should fix Franz. Peter could just see him from the corner of his eye, standing motionless by the door.

Peter suddenly leapt backwards, pulling out his gun. The revolver jumped twice. Franz, a look of surprise on his face, slumped slowly to the ground. The report from the shot was still echoing deafeningly round the room. At the same moment Hank flung himself upon The Counsellor.

"This is it," Peter whispered.

He laid his hand upon the door. Then, above his head, a loudspeaker crackled: "Don't move," a voice purred silkily in English: a cultured, Oxonian voice. "Stay where you are. Another step and you're dead."

The order came from above his head. He looked up at the hidden lattice of the speaker. As he did so his gun was knocked from his hand. Kramer sprang for it and crouched before him, his eyes shining and darting like a wild beast's: the gun barrel wavered from side to side.

"If either of you moves," the silky voice continued, the words echoing round the room, "my men will shoot you down. Eight of my guards have you covered at the moment."

Hank stopped midway in his spring. His knife arm fell to his side.

"Drop your knife, big man."

The voice from the speaker was bantering; the words were echoing silkily round the room and sending shivers down Peter's spine. It was terrifying to be at the business end of eight invisible marksmen... He held his breath.

"Tell them who I am, Ulrich." Once again the loudspeaker crackled. Kramer backed away, pulling the bald man after him.

They stood together behind the desk. A smile was playing at the corners of Kramer's mouth when he spoke.

"*Heil*, Counsellor!" he boomed breathlessly. "You were just in time—" But Kramer kept his eyes fixed upon the two men standing poised in front of him.

"Why did you allow yourself to be captured, Ulrich?" asked the voice from the loudspeaker.

The tone behind the words chilled Peter's blood. He had never heard such a sinister voice. The words poured evilly, like concentrated sulphuric acid. Kramer had gone white: he was sweating and his eyes were wide with terror.

"I tried all I—"

"Don't explain, *Herr Deputy*," the invisible Counsellor interrupted quietly. "I know it all. I've been expecting you. *And* I'm watching you all on closed-circuit television."

Kramer tried to speak as the man at his side slunk behind him. No words would come, and then the loudspeaker snicked again: "The Refuge warned me. They had come to the conclusion that your life was worth risking for the safety of the whole Plan. They summed up the position correctly." The voice paused a moment before continuing slowly, and emphasising each word: "You have arrived earlier than I expected. You, Ulrich, must join me at once. I shall decide what to do with you when I reach The Refuge. There may be use for you even yet. You fool…"

Peter heard the sigh of relief escaping through Kramer's lips. The speaker crackled. The controlled anger had subsided. The voice was now incisive, the words guttural and clipped: "As for the two busybodies, I have no time to bother about them, Ulrich. Arrangements for *Der Tag* are now set in motion. Nothing I can do — no, not even I, The Counsellor — can halt events now. At dawn on the twenty-eighth June, in twenty-eight hours' time, the NATO bombers will be warming up on the tarmac at Rudenfeldt. They'll take off at first light. But amongst the hundreds of planes seven will break formation. They'll turn to the east... Half an hour later the first missiles will be dropping upon Moscow."

The voice was chuckling behind the latticed grille. "Not very difficult, is it, you English busybodies? You probably know the rest... At the identical moment in time, New York will be receiving its ration. That's why I must hurry. The decisions are made, the orders given: the sequence of events is mechanical now. Nothing can halt them."

The Counsellor paused. Peter heard the rustle of movement — a quick whisper. This was the moment Peter had been dodging for so long: the instant of death. He straightened his back. Would the bullets hurt much? Was there much pain? He'd know little ... he *must* do something, he couldn't just *stand* here passively...

"Listen, you madman," Peter shouted upwards at the speaker. "You may have us for mincemeat, but we've got you taped." He paused, his mind racing.

"How so, little man?" The words spilled from the grille. Peter swallowed. He'd better not mention *Rugged*, lying out there in the darkness... She was safe. In an hour or two, Joe Croxton would be informed anyway.

"We know all about you and your organisation. We've been tailing you for months. You're licked — call the whole crazy scheme off."

"I couldn't, even if I wanted to, Englishman. Nothing you or your friends can do can stop us now. We shall be masters of the world in a few days. The New Deutschland..." The words were fanatical in their emotion. "Now I must go." The Counsellor was enjoying himself. "My yacht is waiting in the cove. I must not fall behind schedule. A pity if I was hoisted by my own petard, eh, Englishman? But my U-boat will wait for us off the Balearics."

Peter was in despair. He'd tried, but they'd been outwitted at every turn. Just as well this was the end. There was no future for him or anyone now. The Counsellor was speaking again. His words were curt. "Haven't got time to waste, Ulrich. Leave the room and join me."

Peter watched Kramer take The Counsellor's impostor by the arm and hasten him towards the door. Peter had to step aside to allow them to pass. Kramer's eyes were bright. He spat in Peter's face.

"Go to hell," he hissed. "I win the last trick."

Peter slowly raised his hand to his face. He wiped the spittle from his chin. He was too dejected to care. The door slammed. He turned to look at Hank and their eyes met. Hank's mouth twitched as he tried to smile.

"Raw deal, Pete," he said quietly. "Thanks for bringing me. It was worth trying." He squared his shoulders, looked upwards and closed his eyes.

Peter jumped as the speaker crackled again. "Listen, Englishman. I must not neglect my Henry." The Counsellor's syrupy voice continued. "He and his family are a voracious breed. They thrive on fresh meat. Introduce yourselves. Friends of mine are friends of his. Go on, enjoy the aquarium."

Hank shrugged his shoulders. They walked over to the brick wall. Five yards from it they halted. Below floor level was a circular tank with glass sides. The diameter of the pool must have been at least fifteen feet. The water was illuminated from below. It was this, in combination with some mirror arrangement, that must have been producing the projection of exotic marine life on the back wall.

"Henry is my pet octopus, my friends," The Counsellor was crooning softly. Peter could almost hear him licking his lips. "He has a voracious appetite. I hate abandoning him, but at least I can provide him with one last satisfying meal. He's used to meat at low tide." The Counsellor was chuckling with enjoyment.

"Low water is in three hours' time. He and his family will be hungry." (*He's crazy, a raving fanatic*, Peter thought.) "You'll meet them at low water when the level drops. You see, the tank's connected directly to the sea. Go on — have a look!"

Peter peered over the lip of the tank. The sides were smooth, of some glassy substance. The colours were those of a coral pool, reminding him of Bermuda. There was something weaving to and fro at the bottom of the tank but its outline was still blurred.

"Put on the observation masks by your right hands. You'll see better."

Like the escape tank at Blockhouse, the submarine headquarters in Gosport, Peter thought. He placed the glass flat on the surface of the water and peered through the visor.

The bottom of the tank jumped into focus. And there, pulsating amongst the rocks, was the most repulsive sight Peter had ever seen.

A tangle of tentacles writhed ceaselessly, swaying to the surge of the sea. Grotesque arms were groping upwards towards the light. There must have been several of the brutes. And in the middle of the bulging mass of jelly were two purple stains — the glassy eyes of Henry.

Hank was retching upon the floor. Peter smashed his observation glass against the tank. As he moved to help his friend, he heard a patter behind him. He jerked round too late: half a dozen toughs were toppling them into the tank. The water swirled over his head; the lights went out. Above the pounding of his heart he heard Hank gasping. The threshing of the water slowly subsided until there was a gentle lip-lap against the sides. In the darkness and in the long silence Peter held his breath.

The stillness was shattered suddenly by the laughter of a madman. The echoes rebounded hollowly and slowly died away.

The lip, lip-lapping of the water continued poppling gently against the sides … and all was still.

CHAPTER 18

The Lights Go Out

The Acting Commanding Officer of Her Majesty's Nuclear Submarine *Rugged* felt, like Nelson, justified in disobeying his Captain's orders. This did not make him feel any better as he stood by himself in the darkness on the fin of the submarine.

Taggart was a good officer. Formerly of the R.N.V.R., now reclassified as R.N.R., he had many of the subtler qualities which eluded most Royal Navy officers: in spite of his camaraderie he was sensitive, ultrasensitive almost to a fault. And now, as he saw the lights go out suddenly on the Cap, a strange fear was mounting inside him.

He had always suffered from some sixth sense. (It was this that made him dread the long surface watches of the night.) Now, leaning along the edge of the bridge, his binoculars glued to his eyes, he found his heart pounding against his ribs.

"Keep a good lookout," he snapped. "We've no radar."

The two shadows on either side of the bridge stirred as they dug the eyepieces of their night binoculars more firmly into their eye sockets.

Ian Taggart was worried. All the lights on the islet had gone out too. Perhaps the Captain had thrown the main fuses. Perhaps — no, there was no sane reason for the sudden extinction. He glanced at the luminous dial on his wrist: 0415 — the blackout had lasted over twenty minutes already.

"Dark object, green one-o, sir."

Taggart swung towards the bearing. Stack, the ex-gunlayer, had sharp eyes... Ah! There it was. There, low in the water he saw the white flurry of a bow wave, the dark outline of the folboat. A husky voice hailed from the darkness: "*Rugged* ahoy!"

Taggart leant over and peered down at the blackened face.

"What is it, Hawkins?"

"I reckon the Cap'n's in trouble, sir. All the lights 'ave gorn. And there's somethin' else."

"Yes?"

"There's a yacht slipping out of the cove on the other side."

Taggart felt irritated. Why should that be significant? There were dozens of yachts moored in the coves around the Côte d'Azur at this time of year.

"She's darkened, sir."

That was different! Then Taggart knew what he must do. The Nelson touch was needed here. Sinclair and Jefferson were all he cared about. He'd look after them first — he'd worry about the world afterwards.

He'd land a cutting-out expedition that would include every man-jack, armed to the teeth, that he could spare. O'Donovan could knock up the first telephone and get through to Admiralty. (Surely their Lordships manned an emergency line?) *Rugged* would be safe enough anchored offshore. He could leave her in the capable hands of the Coxswain.

"Stand by to lead us in shore, Hawkins," he called softly towards the canoe in the darkness. "As soon as the landing party's ready, we're coming ashore."

"Hurry, sir. You won't get in very far, though it's almost high-water. For God's sake hurry..."

When Peter had recovered from the shock of the sudden immersion, he found that the enemy, in his haste, had forgotten to disarm them. Though floundering on the surface of the tank, he found himself still clutching the Colt .45. In this darkness there was little use for it, but the feel of it was comforting.

"Hank!"

The splashing to his right had died down. There was a spluttering and snuffling and then the American's voice boomed in the silence. "You okay, Pete?"

Peter dog-paddled towards the voice, his left hand outstretched. "Yep. How about you?"

"Fine."

In the long silence, each knew the other was wrestling with the image awaiting them. Even if they could prevent themselves from drowning (these smooth glass sides gave no hold whatever), those octopi were waiting for the water level to fall with the tide. And if the octopi failed (there seemed to be dozens of them), how could they remain swimming in this tank for another twelve hours, until the following low-water? They'd drown through exhaustion.

"Hank..." Peter hailed softly.

"Yep."

"Come over here."

The splashing came close; Peter could feel the Yank's arm.

"Sorry I got you into this," Peter said. "We walked right into it."

Hank laughed shortly. "Aw, heck. You had no choice. Anyway the main chance is taken care of."

Peter was silent. Yes, Hank could be right; Admiralty would need to verify Taggart's report though. The delay could cost the world its existence.

"There're only twenty-four hours now, before the bombers take off," Peter said.

Hank looked upwards in the domed skylight high above them in the room. He glanced at his waterproof wristwatch: 0417.

"It's getting light, Pete."

Together they watched dawn stealing into the room. A cold light washed the empty room. Now they could see how far the water level had dropped: the lip of the tank was some fifteen feet above them. They couldn't reach it.

"Where d'you reckon The Counsellor's gone, Pete?"

"They've evacuated, lock, stock and barrel. Reckon we interrupted their getaway. They were packed and ready to go."

"Goddam shame. The Refuge was too smart for us. They must have rumbled Kramer's note."

Peter forced a grin in the darkness. He could distinguish Hank's features now.

"We miscalculated on one thing, Hank."

"Yeah?"

"We banked on The Refuge wanting to keep Kramer alive. They didn't give a tinker's cuss: probably preferred him dead."

"Not a popular guy."

Hank grunted: "Pete?"

"Yes."

"I'm touching bottom."

Peter swallowed. The level was dropping fast.

"What's it like?" he asked.

"Feels like rock: a bit slimy. My God, it's draining fast — listen!"

Peter held his breath. Above the surge of the sea he heard the gurgling of water. He looked down.

Dawn was slowly introducing them to their hideous fate. A mass of jelly writhed on the far side of the tank. Something hissed as it whipped across the water.

"Henry's awake." Hank's voice had an edge to it. "A tentacle brushed my leg then, Peter."

Peter felt suddenly the real meaning of terror.

"On our backs, Hank. Keep apart. He won't know who to go for. The other can have the pistol."

Then, floating on his back, he canted his head sideways to have a closer scrutiny.

The rocks were less than three feet beneath them now. His toes felt their sharpness through the slime and the sludge. In the dawn the underwater world was colourless, forbidding and sinister.

A sinuous, clammy-cold softness was washing round his left leg. He felt the tightening, could feel the suckers gripping his flesh; then the irresistible drag downwards.

Peter could not smother the scream on his lips. He dimly remembered his voice reverberating around the tank.

He heard Hank flailing towards him but knew this was the end. He stretched out his arm, holding out the gun, felt Hank grabbing it. Then, as he went under, another snake-like tentacle was groping about his hips. A slimy, cold embrace, wreathing remorselessly around him. He tore at the knife at his side, wrenched it from its scabbard. Then, hysteria gripping him, he lashed out, hacking, slashing, chopping... If Hank got in the way of this blade ... but nothing mattered now. This was his last moment. His lungs were bursting. An inky blackness became his world as dimly his consciousness registered the defence of the octopus. Then, as his brain reeled from the proximity of death, there was a stunning blow against his eardrums — then another and another. Hank was emptying the pistol: too late, too late.

He could breathe no longer; choking, smothered by the water pouring into his lungs. Ah! So peaceful, so quiet — it was over now, quite finished — no longer need he fight, no longer struggle. Why did a man always have to fight? Reminded him of his youth: his mother had always to fight — the Law of Life. Now it was over — done with, finished…

Something hard was clutching his arms. A man's voice, far, far away, shouting in his ears; searing pain beneath his armpits. Lights wheeling and floating; mazy faces peering down at him; hands, many hands, clutching, grappling, passing something rough around him. A face he'd seen before, somewhere, long ago. A seaman's face — ruddy, weather-beaten. Then an American voice, encouraging, kind. Another voice spoke now, a Cockney, kind, gentle and strong…

"'Old fast, sir, 'old on. I've got yer, sir. 'Ave you up in a brace o' shakes."

This was the end of a nightmare: that moment when you jerked back to reality. Didn't they say your past flashed before you as you died? He'd always been fond of Bill Hawkins.

He was choking, unable to breathe now — and then, as he fought for his last breath, he was suddenly breathing air. A long, long draught down to the depths of his lungs; a hot pain in his leg; the release of pressure around his body and then a whirling galaxy of green spinning lights. A roaring about his ears, blackness, spinning … then — nothing more.

CHAPTER 19

Der Tag

At dawn on June 28th, first light was stealing, a silver streak across the eastern sky above the NATO airfield of Rudenfeldt. On the road which ran outside the boundary fence, a Saab screeched to a standstill. Two young men jumped out, staggered for a moment, then ran towards the wire boundary fence of the airfield.

They gripped the chain-fencing as, above the racing of their hearts, they heard the whine of jet engines warming up on the tarmac. The two men began running towards the entrance of the airfield; the larger of the two seemed to be assisting his companion, who was limping. They wheeled into the entrance of the airfield where an American sentry stopped them outside a white guardhouse.

"Sorry, man, you cain't enter without the pass."

Peter Sinclair bit his lip. The bombers would be taking off at any second — and among those bombers lined up on the tarmac were seven traitor pilots.

"Captain Croxton, Royal Navy?" he snapped. "Is he here?"

The sentry looked impressed. "Yeah — drove on to the field twenty minutes ago."

"Get him," Peter shouted. "It's top priority."

The sentry glanced at the Englishman before him. He strolled inside the door, picked up the phone. The roar of the engines was louder now.

"There's two guys here, sir, say they want a Navy Captain...

"Come on, Hank."

Peter started running. He heard Hank pounding after him. Then, as the bullets began whining above his head, he was forced to halt. He shot up his hands.

"Halt you guys!"

Peter turned towards the sentry. He opened his mouth to speak, but no words came. He pointed across the airfield where the roaring of the jets thundered. He heard the familiar whine of a jeep from the shadows, then the slamming of doors beside him.

"Jump in, sir," an American officer shouted. "Captain Croxton's in the tower. He's expecting you."

Hank scrambled into the back and then they were tearing down the runway to the concrete control tower in the middle of the field. The tower loomed out of the gloom. Peter and Hank leaped out and dashed towards the doors where a sentry was waiting to escort them to the lift. But Peter took to the stairs, and thirty seconds later was on the first floor. He burst through the doors marked 'Controller'.

His eyes swept round the circular room: windows along the circumference, a bald-headed man striding purposefully between the scanners. And there, sitting motionless on a stool in the centre of the room, a figure he knew so well.

Joe Croxton turned towards the intruders. His face was drawn, white with fatigue. He nodded at Peter, beckoned them on either side of him. In the silence, Peter tried to quieten his laboured breathing.

"Almost adrift," Joe said.

His face was stern, but there was a high light in those black eyes smouldering in their deep sockets.

"But you're in time to see the finale," he said, nodding towards the lines of fighter-bombers drawn up in threes on the flightpath. "Bomber Command's on the way to Greenland," he added.

Peter was silent. His eyes had become accustomed to the grey light washing Rudenfeldt airfield. The dawn was no different from many in this part of the world: a steely blue-green to the eastward and the morning clouds rolling back below the horizon.

The crescendo of throbbing engines was mounting outside the tower. He could see now the handlers scampering under the wings of the aircraft, the chocks in their hands.

The squadron leader was in the first bomber. Pete saw his raised hand; caught sight of his grotesque martian profile in its oxygen mask as he half-turned towards the tower. The loudspeaker in the Control Room crackled. The men on the scanners crouched low; the murmur of their reports gave reassurance to the strangers' ears.

"Ready for take-off!"

The controller turned towards Captain Croxton. Their eyes met. Joe nodded.

"Scramble!"

Above the sickening whine of the revving jets, Peter heard Joe Croxton shouting at him: "This first squadron are all volunteers for the eastern border sector. The leader's the only one we're sure about — one of our men." Joe turned towards his one-time First Lieutenant. "The rest of the squadrons have been grounded: manned but at stand-by readiness."

That explains it, Peter thought. *That's why the remainder of the aircraft are showing no activity.*

Joe Croxton's face was set hard.

"We called last night for volunteers for the Eastern Border Sector. This is usually an unpopular assignment, but these seven volunteered." He nodded towards the trembling bombers. *"They have orders to fly west until further orders..."*

Joe turned towards Peter. He was shouting now to make himself heard: "If you're right they'll ignore this order: only the leader will continue west. But if you're right..." His outstretched hand swung round the airfield; he was pointing to the woods on the perimeter.

"Ground-to-air batteries..."

He twisted suddenly towards the scream from the jet engines. The high-frequency pitch was nerve-racking.

"There they go!"

The roar of eight jets revving up for take-off reverberated round the room.

The controller stood motionless, watching the sleek arrows streaking down the field. The scanners suddenly crouched lower, their eyes glued to the rotating probes. Their faces were bathed in an eerie green light from the screens. Control now depended entirely upon these operators and, in the right-hand corner of the room, upon another officer. His hand lay poised above a red push-button. As the noise decreased, Peter heard the man speaking:

"All batteries ready, sir. Missiles to Fire." His words were expressionless, calm and flat.

"Start tracking." The controller's order crackled round the room. His voice was tense, irritable. "All batteries stand by."

The last aircraft shuddered, jerked as the brakes loosed her, then swiftly glided down the runway to lift from the ground. She climbed steeply, then suddenly was lost in the dawn cloud. Peter and Hank followed Joe Croxton across to the nearest scanner.

The reports were pouring in from the leader now: "This is Badger One, Badger One — Control. All airborne."

Peter spun round to watch the controller. He was talking in low tones into the mouthpiece of his headset.

"Roger, Badger One. All badgers, *repeat all badgers*, alter course two-seven-zero; repeat, two-seven-zero."

The switch clicked. The steady voice from the ether continued in its flat, unemotional tones.

"*All* badgers, alter course two-seven-zero. Roger, out."

The loudspeaker clicked above their heads, then went dead.

Peter was watching the scanner at his left elbow. He could hear Joe's rapid breathing.

This was the moment of vindication or disaster. If Peter's judgement had been wrong, the calamity would be so catastrophic that not only would Peter's reputation be ruined, but so would Joe Croxton's, the Admiralty's — yes, and the Government's.

But if seven out of those eight bright blips curved to the eastward on the screens...

"Height two thousand..."

"Distance three point two miles..."

"Range four point six miles, sir..."

The reports were coming in fast. "Rangers altering course, sir!"

The report was like a pistol shot. Peter could see the backs of the operators stiffen, watch the muscles tighten in the controller's face. He felt Joe's grip on his arm.

"Look, Peter..." he whispered.

Joe was pointing at the yellow-green Perspex of the scanner.

And there, with one blip continuing firmly on 270°, were a succession of blips curving round to the east.

"Badger one calling rangers, Badger one calling rangers. *Get back on course…*"

The speaker had crackled again. The leader was summoning in angry tones his squadron back into line.

Peter heard the astonishment in the leader's voice, then the ether went dead.

"Rangers steady on o-seven-five, sir. Height three thousand, range five-point-six."

Peter's eyes were on the controller. This was the vital moment. If this man's nerve failed, fourteen H-bombs would be dropping on Moscow in less than twenty minutes. Strange to realise that world conflagration and the fate of mankind lay in this controller's hands…

"Fire!"

Peter jumped. He saw the firing officer jab the red push-button, watched the mauve lights flickering on the panel. Peter turned towards the distant woods.

A sudden silence pervaded the tower — no sound as each soul waited. A smothered cry from the far corner: the controller's head jerking round. All eyes on the windows. There was a blinding light; then an orange-red glow around the eastern circumference of the field. Darkness. A loaded, sudden quiet.

Peter tore his eyes from the windows. The seven blips were streaking across the screen … eastwards. Another few seconds…

Then, pulsating from the horizon, a blue-white flash. Another, then another: blisters of light bursting in the sky to paint the black clouds crimson from the flaming heat.

He held his breath, watching the blips on the screen… Then, as he watched, his heart thumping against his ribs, the first of the yellow smudges vanished slowly from the scan. The image lingered a moment, then disappeared.

Peter stood mesmerised by the screen. Slowly, one by one, like leaves drifting over a weir, the echoes lingered, then vanished…

Peter was rooted to the floor. He stared at the moving banks of cloud. Emotion was choking him and he turned from Joe. Then came the rumble of the explosions from the kill. Joe's hand was on his shoulder.

"Peter, you've done it," Croxton was saying. "But, my God, no one will ever know how close it was. You know one thing, Pete?"

Sinclair shook his head, unable to speak.

"Never again can we allow a fanatic to blackmail the world."

"But who can enforce that?" Peter whispered.

"The United Nations. No one else."

GLOSSARY

AFTER-ENDS — The after section of a submarine.

A.M.C. — Armed Merchant Cruiser.

ASDIC — The device by which submarines are detected. Submarines are also fitted with this device, when it is used as a hydrophone.

BAG — Slang for prisoner-of-war camp.

BARRACK-STANCHION — A man who manages to secure for himself a permanent appointment in a shore station.

BEARING — The direction of an object.

BLOWERS — Machines which blow out the water in the tanks of a submarine by using low-pressure air.

BOX — The main batteries.

BUNCH OF BANANAS — Slang for aiguillettes.

CORTICENE — A type of heavy linoleum used to cover the steel deck.

CRACK — To open a valve quickly, and to shut it immediately.

D.A. — Direction Angle (torpedo-firing angle).

D/EFFED — The bearing of a ship given by her wireless transmission.

D.N.I. — Director of Naval Intelligence.

D.R. — Dead Reckoning.

E-BOAT — The fast enemy motor-torpedo boat.

FIFTH-COLUMNISTS — Traitors working inside one's own society.

FIN — The conning tower of a nuclear submarine.

FORE-ENDS — The forward section of a submarine.

FREE FLOOD — The open holes in the casing and tanks through which the water enters freely.

FRUIT MACHINE — A metal box to which all relevant attack data is fed, and from which the necessary information is extracted to carry out an attack.

GASH — Garbage.

GRATICULE — The fine centre-line and range calibrations which are marked on the lens of the periscope.

GROUP DOWN — Low speed on the main electric motors, thus using up little electric power.

GROUP UP — High speed on the main electric motors, thus using up the battery power quickly.

G.R.U. — *Glavnoye Razvedyvatelnoye Upravlenie* (Chief Intelligence Administration, U.S.S.R.).

GUFF — A squirt of H.P. air.

HEADS — Lavatory.

H.E. — Hydrophone Effect, i.e. propeller noise.

H.E. — High Explosive.

HEAT — Slang for submarine being at the receiving end of a severe depth-charge attack.

H.P. — High Pressure.

H.S.D. — Higher Submarine Detector; the rank of a skilled Asdic operator.

LAYER — A difference of temperature gradients in the ocean.

MAIN BALLAST KINGSTON — Water is allowed to enter into the internal tanks amidships through the Kingston valves.

MAIN BALLAST TANKS — The tanks which give the submarine its buoyancy. All are fitted with main vents, numbers 1 and 6 being external, the remainder internal.

MAIN VENTS — The large mushroom valves on the top of the main ballast tanks. When the main vents are open water will rush into the tanks; but, if the main vents are shut, the air cannot escape when the main ballast tanks are blown, because the 'blow' is at the top of the tank and the free-flood holes at the bottom. Water is therefore forced through the holes in the bottom of the tank, H.P. air taking its place.

N.I.D. — Naval Intelligence Department.

OLD MAN — Slang for Captain.

OUTSIDE E.R.A. — The Engine Room Artificer whose duty is at the panel in the Control Room, and who is therefore 'outside' the Engine Room.

PERISHER — Slang for Commanding Officers' Qualifying Course.

PIFFLE-WURFER — A capsule representing a submarine-contact which can be ejected by a submarine to confuse a destroyer's counter-attack.

PING-RUNNING — Acting as a 'clockwork mouse' to provide a target for training destroyers.

PLUMBER — Slang for Engineer Officer.

PRESSURE HULL — The cigar-shaped hull of a submarine which is tested to the safe diving depth. If any part of this structure is pierced, the submarine is unlikely to survive.

'Q' TANK — The emergency tank for quick diving. When flooded, this extra water makes the submarine heavier than her normal dived trim. After diving, this extra water is blown out of 'Q' tank by high-pressure air. If this tank is required to be flooded when dived, its vent has merely to be opened to allow the air in the tank to be vented either inboard or outboard, when the sea will rush into 'Q'. In wartime 'Q' tank is always kept flooded when the submarine is on the surface.

SCUTTLE — Porthole.

SNOTTY — Midshipman.

STICK — Slang for periscope.

THROWERS — A type of mortar mounted on the quarterdecks of destroyers. When fired they hurl depth charges well clear of each quarter.

U-BOAT — Enemy submarine of any nationality.

UCKERS — The sailor's version of 'Ludo'.

URSULA SUIT — Waterproof overalls in general use, designed by the Commanding Officer of H.M. Submarine *Ursula*.

A NOTE TO THE READER

Dear Reader,

If you have enjoyed the novel enough to leave a review on **Amazon** and **Goodreads**, then we would be truly grateful.

Sapere Books is an exciting new publisher of brilliant fiction and popular history.

To find out more about our latest releases and our monthly bargain books visit our website:
saperebooks.com